T

IN

FLINT

THROUGH PARTS OF

SOUTH WILTSHIRE

IN

1808

WRITTEN IN

𝔄 𝔖𝔢𝔯𝔦𝔢𝔰 𝔬𝔣 𝔏𝔢𝔱𝔱𝔢𝔯𝔰

IN WHICH ARE DESCRIBED; THE ACQUIRING OF A
SNAKECATCHER'S HAT, THE RESURRECTION OF DON
QUIXOTE OF LA MANCHA, A TRANSACTION WITH
MR. HENRY SHORTO, ESTEEMED CUTLER OF SALISBURY,
A SINGLE STICK CONTEST INVOLVING THE EXTRAORDINARY
MR. WILLIAM HAZLITT AT THE WINTERSLOW HUT,
AND A SOURCE FOUND OF THE HIGHEST QUALITY **FLINT** AND
EVIDENCE OF ITS EXTRACTION BY ANCIENT MAN.

BY

A PEDESTRIAN. [Nich. Cowen]

EAST KNOYLE :

PUBLISHED BY THE HOBNOB PRESS

2009.

☞ *First published in 2009 by The Hobnob Press, PO Box 1838, East Knoyle, Salisbury SP3 6FA.*

© *Nick Cowen ('A Pedestrian') 2009.*

☞ *All illustrations are by the author.*

☞ *British Library Cataloguing in Publication Data: A catalogue record for this book is available from the British Library.*

ISBN 978-0-946418-75-6.

☞ *Typeset in Bodoni and designed by John Chandler.*

Printed in Great Britain by Antony Rowe Ltd.

A TOUR IN SEARCH OF
CHALK

Through parts of South Wiltshire
IN 1807

BY A PEDESTRIAN

South Wiltshire and its characters form the backdrop
for young Londoner Henry chalk on his *first* pedestrian
adventure as he puts pen to paper his travails are recounted
and his own story unfolds.

ENCOUNTERING ON THE WAY;

A CHARCOAL BURNER IN GROVELY WOOD; A GATHERING OF
ANTIQUARIANS AT STONEHENGE; A DARING ENTRANCE TO FONTHILL
ABBEY AND A MISUNDERSTANDING WITH THE CALIPH OF FONTHILL-
MR WILLIAM BECKFORD; ELECTION NIGHT AT HINDON WHERE A
CHANCE ENCOUNTER WITH A YOUNG WOMAN TENDS TO TRUE LOVE;
AN INVITATION TO STOURHEAD HOUSE AS A GUEST OF SIR RICHARD
COLT HOARE; A BARROW "OPENING" UPON WHITESHEET HILL AND,
FINALLY, INCRIMINATION FOR OUR YOUNG HERO AFTER THE DISCOVERY
OF A BODY UPON THE ROAD IN THE EARLY MORNING.

YOUNG HENRY CHALK is torn between his responsibilities
at the family brewery in Southwark and a taste for adventure.
Inspired by his uncle, who published an account of his own .

[pedestrian . . .

. . . own]

pedestrian excursion in North Wales in 1805, the young nephew follows suit, unaware that such publications were often plagiarised from the accounts of others.

The discovery of an ancient flint weapon by Henry Chalk from the Fisherton brickearth, upon his arrival in Salisbury, and subsequent flint tools recovered from the plough-soil lead to bold and unconventional thoughts upon the distant history of this land and its inhabitants. Can the young Pedestrian convince Sir Richard Colt Hoare, the author of a seminal work – *"The Ancient History of Wiltshire"* – the import of these discoveries?

PRICE £7.95

DEDICATION.

MY PARENTS: NICK AND FREDA

LETTER TO THE EDITOR

THE EARLIER PUBLICATION of my nephew's letters to myself entitled "A Tour In Search Of Chalk" has not engendered the expected response from its author Mr Henry Chalk and, as a consequence, I have been unable to establish his whereabouts and thereby ensure his wellbeing to my satisfaction. South Wiltshire does indeed appear to hold some fascination for my young and naive relative and provides fertility to his imagination for it is only when he is at large in that place that the ink flows from his pen. I know of no other means to ensure contact other than to replicate the earlier method and publish a further flood of these letters from the same itinerant source. The noblemen and gentlemen who have deemed it their responsibility to befriend my nephew have thus far been ungraciously reticent to my direct pleas to encourage our reunion and I believe that they are stifling my requests for contact to the extent of withholding my correspondence.

His responsibilities in life are clear and simple and as his sole surviving relative it is my avuncular duty to provide the <u>correct</u> guidance. Chalk's brewery in Southwark, London is thriving with its new source of water and yet the trustees are desperate for its young heir to take up his position at the helm as is only proper and correct.

As a plea to the general reading public I shall offer, through my publisher, a reward of TWENTY GUINEAS to whosoever can provide information that leads directly to the location of HENRY CHALK — PEDESTRIAN TOURIST.

Yours faithfully
J. CHALK
July 1808

From the Editor
The following V pages of
incomplete correspondence, dated
January 1808, are hereby offered to the
reader as an INTRODUCTION to the noble
and worthy antiquarians, so oft referred to,
in "A Tour in Search of Flint".

January 1808.

. . . blankets pulled across our laps in the carriage. Mr Fenton rubbed at the glass to survey our progress and then proclaimed grandly that in his opinion it would snow before noon and to confirm this view he fully pulled down the carriage window and savoured the air. There was some resistance to this action by Mr John Fenton who hurriedly buried himself deeper under the blanket; "Father you may travel on the roof if you wish to become better acquainted with the weather but please spare us the icy blasts." Mr Cunnington and Sir Richard Colt Hoare were not to be so easily distracted from their lengthy discussion regarding the various forms of disease that torment the Wiltshire sheep population and after refastening the window Mr Fenton expelled a long sigh and then directed his attention towards myself. "There has to be somebody amongst us who can display even the smallest degree of excitement at the prospect of today's antiquarian entertainment? John is for cowering under a blanket all the while since our departure from Heytesbury whilst our host and patron have explored the defects in every part of the anatomy of the poor afflicted sheep.

As a result I never again wish to encounter mutton at the end of my fork. Please Mr Pedestrian are you able to rescue us from this most desperate of situations."

I did my best to reassure Mr Fenton that indeed we would not have been so readily drawn from our respective hearths and travelled no small distance if there were not a quorum of wholehearted support for this venture. Privately, My dear Uncle, I had wondered beforehand at the wisdom of this visit to the south of the Salisbury Plain for this was to be a barrow "opening" out of season with it being just nine days into the new year. The Baronet and Mr Richard Fenton depart for London in the morning and are not to return until the spring and I wonder at Sir Richard Colt Hoare's health for I have been kept abreast of his poorly condition over these last months. Mr William Cunnington is still plagued by the severest of headaches for which at their onset, only rest and darkness offer some eventual relief.

I can report from my fireside at the Deptford Inn that all appeared well at our parting at the end of the day but, as I shall soon conclude my account, the visit to the Ashton Valley barrow cemetery did not reap its expected reward. Tomorrow Mr John Fenton and myself return from whence we came to Fishguard and whilst my cold fingers grapple with the pen my fellow traveller is warming his own hands by the throwing of the dice at the next table.

On our way to the Ashton Valley and its companion the gentle Chitterne Brook we first passed through the village of Codford St Peter and were then obliged to depart from the decent toll road. It was at this junction that Mr Richard Fenton brought his hands together with such a crack that even our host and patron ceased their bucolic exchange. As the carriage rocked to and fro and having now gained all our attentions, Mr Fenton addressed the party; "Yes gentlemen it is gold that we crave, no broken urn or rusting blade.." his voice rose to compete with the grinding of the carriage wheels across loose stone ".. with the leaves of gold that shone ..on the Arch-druids's breast alone, when his office bade him GO . . . TO CUT THE SACRED MISTLETOE . . " Before the conclusion of this verse I was fully thrown from my seat by the lurching of the carriage and was caught in the arms of the two Mr Fentons. Mr Cunnington rapped with the butt of his stick to alert the driver to restrain the horses and quickly apologised to the party for this extreme discomfort. Mr Richard Fenton then sank back into his seat pulling the blanket toward him and complained that he had been unfairly defeated from delivering his soliloquy by the incommodious nature of the road and the moment having passed he would now sit in silence with a request that he should not be disturbed.

I confess that I find Mr Fenton's antics of constant amusement and I cannot keep a smile from my face when I am present in his company. Sir Richard Colt Hoare patted his friend upon the knee and commiserated at the untimely interruption but he then added in seriousness that " We are not a band of treasure hunters and it is enough for a barrow to divulge its secrets whatever those might be and it is our antiquarian duty to record all that we may find."

It is my understanding, my dear Uncle that Mr Fenton's anticipation was not unfounded. Not five years ago Mr Cunnington's men opened a barrow in the village of Upton Lovell that was situated next to the river Wylye and the object of today's attention in the Ashton Valley was similarly placed beside the lapping waters of the Chitterne Brook. From the great "Golden Barrow" at Upton Lovell, for that has become its nomenclature, many rare golden objects were retrieved and I wonder that it is the draw of this precious metal that has brought us all to the skirts of Salisbury Plain in the heart of winter. Mr Cunnington has on four earlier occasions instructed his men to delve into this Ashton Valley barrow, the largest of the group, but without success so today was to be the fifth attempt. I cannot believe that there is any burial mound within the scope of this expert team that has received so much attention or so many visits.

As I have now become accustomed to find at such proceedings, our arrival at the barrow was coincident with the result of a mornings toil by Mr Cunningtons' two labourers Stephen and John Parker who are a team of Father and Son. To fulfil Mr Richard Fenton's earlier prediction a fine mist of snow began to fall and quickly deposited small flakes of white upon the garments of our party as we eagerly gathered to hear the news from Mr Cunnington's men. We were led to the southern side of the barrow where a small cist had been uncovered in the native chalk. It was apparent that great care had been displayed in its excavation with the application of a small trowel and Mr Stephen Parker now used this tool to direct our attention toward its content. My dear Uncle, I do not consider that I have experienced a greater silence as we looked down upon the skeleton of a child of perhaps no more than twelve months in age. The falling snow soon thickened and made a veil where only moments earlier nearby hills had formed the horizon and it was as if we had become detached from the rest of the world. Our antiquarian zeal had now of a sudden become sombre and funereal for we all in turn bowed our heads and, following the example of the two Mr Parkers, we then removed our hats. Sir, I believe that each and every family has been visited by the tragedy of a young life unfulfilled and we all harbour the deepest sadness of such a memory within our hearts. The bold flakes now shrouded the excavation and it was left to Sir Richard Colt Hoare to break the silence.

"How many is that now Mr Cunnington?" Mr Cunnington replied that there had been eleven interments of burned bones and now two skeletons.

"It is perhaps a family mausoleum is it not?.." concluded the Baronet "..and no treasure for you Mr Fenton."

"Indeed not Sir.." agreed his good friend "..for it was surely a poor and overcrowded family".

Mr Cunnington gave a signal for the two labourers to . . .
(End of incomplete chapter, Editor)

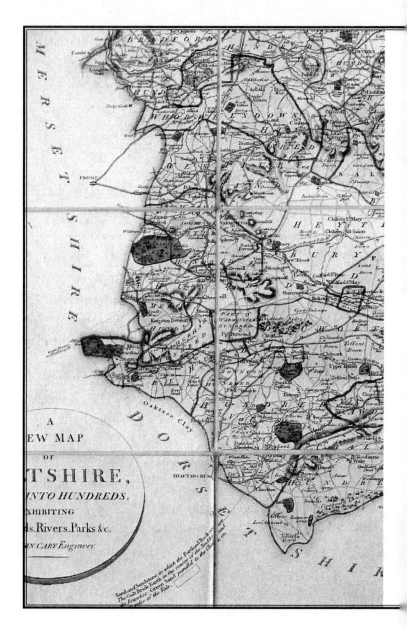

Part of Mr Cary's Map of Wilt-

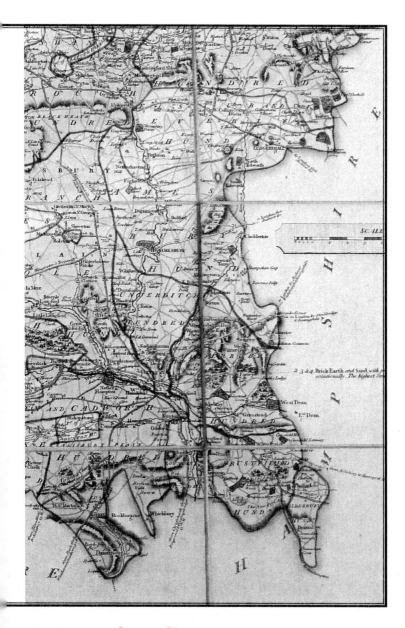

shire, shewing the Southern Parts thereof

Friday May 6th 1808

MY DEAR UNCLE,

With my crossing again into the county of Wiltshire I am back
with pen in hand. There is a palpable eruption of the earth's
goodness through every unfurling and trembling shoot and
indeed the birds and mammals need no convincing of these
issues for there is both a bold and furtive activity on land, air
and water.

I write these words beside the River Nadder whose sandy
waters contain the secrets of the steep and wooded slopes of
this vale. There is a tree that appears to thrive on its proximity
to the river here, it has a dark waxy green leaf and its roots
cling to these soft banks in knotted desperation. Under just
such a tree I have sought some welcome shade for today
is exceedingly warm and having removed my pack I sense
the wetness of my labours thus far upon my back and I feel
justified in stripping down to my shirt.

How can I apologise to you Sir, not only for the great
trouble I have caused you but also for the neglect in not
communicating my whereabouts these last few months? I
made one brief excursion into South Wiltshire in January and
I even recorded the details of the occasion in an unsent letter
to you. I then dispensed with some pages of pathetic apology
and abandoned the correspondence and I still struggle to find

the words to make good and explain my behaviour. You will surmise that I have not yet returned to my duties in London for which I am ashamed. I hold no doubt though that the business of beer is prospering for it is not waning in fashion nor is it a thirst that will ever be quenched.

On departing from Wiltshire last October I retreated to the coast of Pembrokeshire in South Wales at the invitation of Mr Richard Fenton and was made most welcome at his family home in the town of Fishguard. I have spent some weeks employed in the task of making orderly the affairs of Mr Fenton where he has fishing boats and also property in the harbour. My host has some business but he is no businessman and it is a failing to which he readily admits. I have been able to set in motion some improvements to the maintenance of the properties that were suffering from neglect. I can hear you suggest, my dear Uncle, that if I am happy to labour behind a desk in Fishguard then surely I can assume my responsibilities at Chalk's brewery in Southwark? In my heart I know that once I return I shall never leave and as a consequence I am not yet fit to do so.

Mr Fenton has spent a deal of time in London as a companion to his good friend Sir Richard Colt Hoare but family life at Glynamel, Mr Fenton's home, has been a succour to me and I have been able to straighten my senses a little. I still have two major preoccupations. The first is of a romantic nature and you will not be surprised to learn that Miss Sarah Foster has a firm hold on my heart and by necessity all our correspondence is directed through her brother Robert. Without Robert we would be lost for he commits to the page his sister's thoughts and from his lips my words are transmitted in return. Whilst I am unable or unwilling to settle I cannot be introduced to the Foster household yet Robert deems me trustworthy and honourable in my intentions towards his sister for our communications to continue. When Robert is absent, as he is presently, then our intimate thoughts remain unwritten and unread so I have chosen to embark again on a short pedestrian tour of South Wiltshire to occupy my mind. Indeed I have arranged to meet with Robert Foster in seven days time at the Winterslow Hut which is situated on the London road some miles to the east of Salisbury. Robert is returning from London on his way back to the family home in Minehead and it has been agreed that we should make our first acquaintance with one another, a meeting to which I am greatly looking forward.

I list two preoccupations my dear Uncle and the latter will also fail to surprise. The former I have explained and the second could not offer more opposing properties for it is the hard and cold flint that abounds in this county. Sir you have been the recipient of the accounts of my earlier rummaging through the soils of Stourhead to retrieve examples of fashioned flint and it is a subject on which I have puzzled at great length. I carry some of the finer pieces around with me along with the flint weapon from the Fisherton brickearth. Whilst I dwell on geological matters, I also have a fragment from one of the smaller upright stones that I found detached upon the ground on my visit to Stonehenge. It is however the pursuit of flint of the richest quality that has brought me back to Wiltshire and Mr Richard Fenton would suggest in all seriousness that I had embarked upon "A Tour in Search of Flint..etc..etc". Sir, my aims are modest ones and I am reticent even to impose them upon your patient self and not, as my good friend would recommend, to broadcast them to the whole wide world.

I shall now continue my pedestrianism and I will take my time for what would there be to report if, after a hearty breakfast at dawn and with head down and elbows out to the sides, I should be beyond the county boundary by dusk. I prefer to sit and stare, to circle a hill before ascending it, to stand without boots and stockings in a clear stream and to creep up and ensnare a view with my pencil. It is ponderous but it is all at a pace that permits observation. For now Sir I wish you the very best of good afternoons for there is no untruth, that I can detect, in that statement.

*

I have tarried again on my journey and I realise my dear Uncle that I do not even possess a watch so I can only judge the time by the positioning of the sun. I have placed myself before an old ruin with pencil in hand and in that duration the shadows here have lengthened and I would gauge that it is now perhaps five o clock. I have yet to truly complete any drawing in my life and I make no exception here but this scene of crumbling strength, now crowned with a neglect of ivy, is a model of the picturesque which even Mr Gilpin's critical eye may approve. There is a wondrous stillness here broken only by a stark cawing on my arrival of a large black bird that dwells in the upper reaches of this place. As I settled to my task the only movement and sound became the passing of lead from pencil to paper and I have been lost under the spell of great concentration.

Forgive me Sir for I am a distracted traveller and I have neglected to describe my route thus far. Mr John Cary's map is still in my possession and I have flattened it out before me upon the grass. I see that this place is called Wardour and there is a grand new property not a mile away with its fresh white stone shining in the evening sun. Sadly Mr Cary's map can only inform of villages and their connecting roads and does not contain sufficient detail to negotiate the web of paths and feint trails that thread across this most mysterious quarter of Wiltshire. This is not chalk country but heavy land that holds water with small fields and flourishing hedges with many marshy places. On leaving the hilltop town of Shaftesbury I met again with the green sands that I first encountered in Stourhead on the estate of Sir Richard Colt Hoare. Indeed there is a ridge at a place called Wincombe where on its steep northern slopes great excavations have been made that must surely have provided a great deal of the large green blockstone for that nearby town. Today these giant scars have been healed over by a cloak of trees and low tangled growth but I wonder at the immense scale of this operation and at man's tireless ability to plunder any useful resource. I then descended a dank and dark stony way with many plants of a lush greenness upon each bank. They prosper well in this shade and must feed upon the many water seepages here on these slopes and I noted the appearance of a deep yellow ochre clay on my boots. Upon reaching the base of the valley I crossed a stream where both man and beast have left their mark in the bankside mud; a bootprint and a cloven hoof side by side. A street or a cobbled road does not spark this deep reminder that we share this earth with our silent partners, yet today my own buried senses have been stirred by this close proximity to nature. I have followed paths not created solely by the padding of human feet for they are also coincident with the passing of smaller creatures; A gathering of fur upon a bramble, a rank scent in the air, a dark stool deposited in a shallow scraping and signs of burrowing and homebuilding nearby.

At the crossing of field boundaries there are wooden rails with also a simple wooden step set across these footpaths and the sighting of which aids ones progress as to the way ahead. The top bar of these structures are made smooth by use, oiled by the palms of country hands and then buffed to a gloss by the seats of many pairs of Wiltshire breeches. I observed the human users of these paths from a distance as I am uncertain of my own entitlement to follow. I have greeted oncoming walkers with politeness by raising my hat but I understand by the curious expressions on these faces that they know that I am a stranger who passes this way but once. In the farmyards and the fields there is much activity. Cows are led to feed upon the bright grass by calling boys with whipsticks whilst gangs of men are digging at the steaming dung in the cattle pens in the yards, heaping it up and throwing it aboard open carts with long forks and it is then hauled away. In a cultivated field I have seen rows of men and women upon their knees picking at the small weeds. In another field a plough is drawn by a team of two set one before the other turning a narrow ridge of soil with unerring straightness.

Today the River Nadder has been my faithful companion from its infancy near Shaftesbury and it has led me in turn through the villages of Donhead st Mary and Donhead st Andrew. I have observed its opaque waters gushing at two old greenstone mills whilst I myself have been observed by two suspicious millers. I finally abandoned my friend the river at the first sight of the Wardour ruin and by skulking across open parkland and around small lakes in my quest to reach this place, I have splashes of mud and clay up to my knees which will not endear me to any respectable innkeeper.

Not only does Mr John Cary's map accompany me to Wiltshire but also the charcoal burner's azel stick has made its return after a dormant winter. I thought it dry and lifeless in the hallway in Pembrokeshire but now I believe it would sprout fresh growth if it were able such is the keenness it displays probing and tapping the ground and flicking at thorn wands that threaten to snag at my stockings. I have thought much about Peter Winter and the boy Tam but I shall resist disturbing their business in Grovelly for I am determined not to become entangled in the lives of others but shall keep my own company. The arrival of evening at my ruin has brought a succession of visitors in their carriages and I believe that it is time for me to depart although I may enquire of a nearby inn that would welcome a mud splashed pedestrian tourist.

*

Sir, how a mood can change in a day. On my arrival at the Glove Inn, which is situated on the turnpike at the foot of a steep escarpment and not two miles from the Wardour ruin, I was greeted with indifference by the landlord. I have a small room to myself and have now eaten a moderate supper and there should be little out of the ordinary to report. It has not been so. I had not even been escorted to my room when in a passageway I was confronted by Mr William Beckford's diminutive servant who recognised me in an instant and then barred my way with feet apart and hands on hips. His voice chilled me for it is a rasping growl and it brought back the horrors of my foolish venture to Fonthill and the resulting pursuit in the village of Hindon. "Well, well, well, look and see it is the trespass boy." He then turned and beckoned with a stumpy finger for me to follow and I felt helpless to do otherwise. He showed me to a side room and gestured for me to enter and he then repeated his initial greeting for the benefit of the occupants inside. Seated in two padded chairs on either side of the window were Mr William Beckford and another gentleman whom I did not recognise and I was ushered further into the room by the little servant as he pushed the door closed behind him. Mr William Beckford viewed me in silence for a moment before addressing the other seated gentleman; "Franchi, please permit me to introduce to you a young man whose identity has never been established. Trespass is a serious matter and our nameless friend here, on October last, entered my property under a cloud of misunderstanding which he made no attempt to dispel. Instead he scampered up the tower like a town rat and then fled the building and Mr Dwarf suffered at my own hand as a consequence." The second gentleman did not address me directly and with a feint foreign flavour to his voice he enquired of Mr Beckford what was to become of this intruder. The owner of Fonthill Abbey considered the matter for a moment and drummed his fingers together under his chin as if fidgeting whilst at prayer "I believe it calls for official proceedings, this instant and in this very room." He then issued highly pitched and sharp commands to his scowling servant to rearrange the dining chairs so that three were placed behind the table with one remaining on the opposing side. I was then instructed to put down my pack and stick and take my position upon the single chair whilst the other three gentlemen aligned themselves before me across the table with Mr Beckford in the centre. "Mr Dwarf would you gather the pen and paper from that worm eaten writing desk.. Franchi you shall make a record of the proceedings ..and so, in this filthy place that is but a

rustic brothel, let us commence." Mr Beckford rapped upon
the table with his knuckle and pronounced that the court was
now in session and then turned his penetrating gaze upon me
before requesting my name and address to which I dutifully
responded.

"Mr Henry Chalk you stand accused of trespassing in the
grounds and property of Mr William Beckford of Fonthill,
how do you plead?"

I tried to gather my thoughts. From outside in the
courtyard the regular beat of a blacksmith's hammer upon his
anvil grew louder in my mind " tink ..tink..tink..tink.. tink..
tink.." until it became the mechanism of some great ticking
clock and in my confusion time flew, ebbed and then stopped
still altogether as the blacksmith ceased in his labours.

"Is he dead?" asked the gentleman called Franchi.

"I do not believe so" advised Mr Beckford.

"Ee is stupeed?" suggested the dwarf.

Finally the words gushed forth and I was able to explain
the circumstances that led to my unauthorised entry and the
making against my will of the wager with Mr John Fenton. It
was established that I had profited to the sum of five guineas
by which time I sat with my head bowed at the unravelling of
this foolishness.

"Are these somewhat pathetic excuses now duly recorded
Franchi?"

"Yes your worshipful majesty and lordship."

The judge in this mock courtroom then requested that I

take my chair with me and sit out in the passageway whilst a verdict is reached and my guilt established to which I tamely obeyed.

How long I sat with my back to the wall in a listless torpor I know not. I heard a coach clatter into the yard and a hubbub of activity ensued and I was soon required to tuck in my feet as the passengers then trailed passed my position in the hallway, noisy and impatient and with the odour of having been confined in close proximity on a hot day. There appeared to be a collective anxiety about what lay ahead in the dining room and would there be a meal prepared in readiness? Would there then be sufficient time to eat this undoubtedly costly meal and still return to the carriage to retain a favoured seat? Age or sex presented no barriers to the ambitiously hungry for there was a great amount of jostling on the way to the table. The call of "All ready" by the coachman was greeted by cries of distress by the only partially fed as they stole away with anything that could be carried from the plate with the landlord in pursuit " Oi you brings that back!" My feet received another trampling in the race back to the coach and with more jeering and calling their journey continued and in a short while all was silent again.

A service maid passed me and before I was able to state that the gentlemen within did not wish to be disturbed she proceeded to open the door to the side room. The maid gave me a curious look and demonstrated that the room was now empty and sure enough on my inspection the furniture had been restored to its original position and it contained no persons at all. The maid retrieved my chair from the hall and placed it before the table, she then departed through another door that I had not noticed in a panelled wall that led through to the parlour leaving me alone to collect my pack and my stick. So Mr William Beckford and his men have had their fun with me and I cannot say that I did not deserve it. Whilst I sat forlornly in the passageway they silently departed through another exit, no doubt with much amusement. The landlord later informed me that their purpose at the inn was unusual and was caused only by Mr Beckford's horse throwing two shoes as they descended White Sheet Hill and indeed it was the farrier's blows that I could hear. My timely appearance it seems has supplied the three gentlemen with some idle amusement whilst the son of Vulcan carried out his work at the forge.

I believe that my supper was first served up late to the agitated passengers of the evening stage who had not the time to enjoy it and I derived little pleasure at my turn with it. I have ended the day with my spirit crushed when previously before my arrival at this place it had been soaring with the sights and sounds of my return to Wiltshire. My thoughts shall now retreat to a place that always brings me hope and courage and I bid you goodnight.

Your errant nephew
HENRY CHALK.

MY DEAR UNCLE,

I am now aware of the punishment that Mr Beckford and his men have inflicted upon me after their holding of a mock court at the Glove Inn. On leaving that place with a desire to reunite myself with the chalk and ascend the steep ridge that rises up above the Glove Inn I found that my azel stick had been fractured in the middle. I had not noticed last night as I was downcast and still smarting from the humiliation of my unwelcome encounter with the owner of Fonthill Abbey but as soon as it struck the turnpike this morning my stick buckled beneath me. Whilst I had been banished to the passageway I did not hear the crack of the stick across the little servant's knee for it was surely he that executed the punishment. It is only a stick and there are plenty more to be had in the thickets and hedgerows but it is a cruel thing to inflict upon a pedestrian tourist and I hope that this shall be the end of the matter.

There is a tollgate at the foot of the downs and the road from Salisbury now avoids the perilous descent down this spine of chalk that bears the name of White Sheet Hill. The old trackway forms a conspicuous chalk scar and has a rocky water worn surface and it is here last evening that Mr Beckford's horse lost two of its shoes. I believe that this cleft in the chalk was not so naturally formed as it first appeared to me for it bears the signs of its construction as a highway. Upon the banks in the field on the lower side there are great spoil heaps now grassed over and also there are cuts through this lower bank to discharge the rain water. Considerable excavation has taken place here in a battle against the natural form of the land in order to make this way passable and less precipitous but the creaking wheels have now abandoned this road and it is left in neglect for the more adventurous traveller. I write these words at the very crest of White Sheet Hill for I have not yet travelled any distance at all on this hot morning before placing myself down upon an ancient burial mound that Mr Cunnington, a man whom I respect greatly for his judgement and reason in these matters, would term a "long barrow". It is yet another display of man's desire to make their mark upon the chalklands but in this instance it is the work of our ancient ancestors and its purpose is I believe sacred and not a matter of utility. I hold no doubt that beneath my seated position at the higher eastern end of this mound lie the bones of a people who lived in an age before the advent of metal. Mr Cunnington has informed me that no metal objects have ever been retrieved in their examination and I therefore surmise that these are indeed the most ancient of all the tombs that abound in the south of this county. It is a life wholly dependent upon the utility of flint that draws me to the creators of these fine and elegant Long Barrows. I can only wonder where these mysterious people obtained the stone that was essential to their every need. The natural and weathered flint that lays in abundance amongst the chalky plough soil is not to be compared with the rich and dark material of which their early tools are manufactured.

I can see a distant tree clump upon the horizon that shall be my next goal and it is a landmark that has already gained my attention for I viewed it yesterday from the Donhead villages. My spirit has been restored and I shall cast my eye about for a suitable replacement for Peter Winter's stick. I have been loath to part with it this morning but what use is a broken stick to a pedestrian tourist?

*

With my landmark before me I then set out across the closely cropped grass and I determined that I would not fill my head with noble thoughts but instead crave a greater lightness of spirit. Sarah does tease me in her letters that I have the gravitas of one who is at the end of life's journey and not one who is just setting out and so I began to sing aloud a song of nonsense to help me along. I was not overheard in my foolishness or silenced by some brooding thought but by the twinkling sounds of an invisible flock whose magical song descended from the heavens like the faint chiming of tiny bells. I stopped and guarded my eyes against the morning's brightness and studied the clear blue sky but still could not detect the originators of this mysterious birdsong that accompanied me to the foot of the chalk slope. Here I again met with the sandy green soils that appear to exist beneath the chalk and I traversed around the grounds of a large house that barred my progress. Towering trees were alive with spurting bright green leaf and as I walked in their flickering shade I spied a piece of paper lying on the wayside amongst the fresh grass. I retrieved the folded page and I was drawn to read, with mounting guilt, the most intimate of letters between two young people in love and estranged by distance to which I had an immediate empathy. This final sheet of correspondence was signed "Percy Bysshe" and the eloquence of these most sensitive words and verse made me halt. I read the page again with no more pangs of guilt but just wonderment, and I believe envy, that these were not my own words. A fat pigeon clopped its wings together as it left a perch above my head and I am now very thankful to that bird for it broke my reverie and got my feet in motion again for at that moment a young woman appeared on the path ahead of me. Here surely was the recipient of the letter and I have not at all been a gentleman in spying upon their love. I could not now cast the page back onto the verge for we were too close and this action would have been conspicuous. Instead I folded it in two and pretended to stoop to retrieve it from the ground and I would be seen to carry out this movement without the time to be aware of its content. I cannot pretend my dear Uncle for this deception has left me feeling that I am the worst kind of person and I flush with some embarrassment at my own actions as I write these words. As we drew close I removed my hat and bid the young lady good morning whilst I also held out the folded page. Before I could enquire as to whether she may have suffered the loss of a scrap of paper the young lady instantly recovered it from my grasp with a snap of her wrist and she then held it tightly to her breast.

"Thank you, it is private correspondence and I did not realise that I had mislaid it." I introduced myself and declared my purpose as a pedestrian tourist. The young lady did not reciprocate but instead looked at me askance and said; "So you are not a vagabond then? I should like to continue with my business and your business appears to require the taking of a liberty by walking on my father's property, that of Mr Thomas Grove of Ferne and we should be gratified if you do not pass this way again. Good morning Mr Chalk." I assured the young lady that I would pass this way but once when in truth my dear Uncle I had doubly trespassed for I had entered upon the intimate affairs of her heart and to tread upon such sensitive ground is surely the more unforgivable. As we parted the young lady then paused and called back "Pedestrians would not be welcome upon the Chase either as you seem to be venturing in that direction. Should Lord Rivers' men catch up with you then you can expect no quarter."

I made the long and hot ascent to my goal not thinking of warnings or admonishments or even the wretchedness of prying upon the intimate lives of others but instead of the rich poetry and incendiary language of one who signed himself "Percy Bysshe".

It seems that I have made more use of my pen than my
boots on this morning but I believe that it is not unreasonable
to seek shelter from the ferocity of this sun. My clump of trees
smells strongly of the residue of the shepherds flock but it is a
vantage point that demands time of the viewer and indeed the
landscape can be made some sense of now that I have looked
up from my writing. I can see my trail thus far this morning
and I can also detect the glinting of some shiny object upon
the distant long barrow.

*

I am now installed at the Woodyates Inn. Night comes with
some relief from the relentless sun for today it has surely
scorched my skin. It is not as cool as night should be for my
window is wide open and it is a warm breeze that plays with
the candle. I shall sleep with a single sheet when I reach my
bed but there is still much to recount and I hope Sir that you
will forgive my indulgence.

I must begin with the telling of a woeful tale about my
own carelessness and the loss of something very precious.
On the advent of my 18th birthday I was presented with a
portable eyeglass by Mr Richard Fenton. It was indeed an
unexpected and handsome gift contained within its own black
shark skin case. It has seven draw tubes and alongside the
makers name there is inscribed "Mr Henry Chalk-pedestrian
tourist". With this instrument I have scoured the wild ocean
from the Pembrokeshire cliffs in search of sea tossed ships
and it has also accompanied me to the barren mountains of

Prescilli. I used it yesterday to view my tree clump from the
Donhead villages and this morning, from the long barrow, I
spied upon the progress of the building of the tower of Fonthill
Abbey before turning my back on that place. I wished to use
it to establish the origin of the glinting object that caught my
attention but I could find only the black carry case in my pack.
The cause of this shining was none other than the lens of my
own spyglass flashing in the sunlight yet it was not dancing
about on its own upon the long barrow for it is now in the hands
of another. Upon this realisation I felt giddy with distress and
paced about awaiting further flashes as a confirmation of my
loss. I resolved to retrace my steps as swiftly as I was able
and I stowed my pack and even my coat amidst dense cover
and taking only my water bottle I scrambled back down the
steep and grassy slopes. You will gather from my frustrations
that all my haste and exertions were in vain for as the long
barrow eventually came into view I could see no figure upon
its summit and on my arrival I found neither my spyglass nor
indeed even my broken thumbstick. I then returned to the
Glove Inn to report this loss and also to ask of the landlord
to be vigilant should he see or hear of anything that might
lead to the recovery of such a precious object. A silver coin
affected I believe only a temporary interest in my plight and
I left after informing him that I should be at the Winterslow
Hut on the London road in five days time. I drank deeply
from the well in the yard and refilled my water flask before a
slow and weary return to my belongings upon the hill. I was

gratified that the daughter of Ferne did not reappear before me for I had boldly promised to pass through the grounds of that place only once and not thrice as misfortune had now dictated.

I resolved to continue my journey in an easterly direction along the grand and undulating chalk ridge for I did not wish to again relinquish the advantage of this hard won elevation. To the south of my position I could see across great portions of the county of Dorsetshire until land and sky met on hazy and indistinct terms which it seems is a general accompaniment to a blazing sun. In time I absently deviated from my course and began a slow descent amidst a large tract of woodland with all the while a distracted mind for company and a growing unease that I was somehow being observed. For want of any other possibility my imagination had now contrived that Mr Beckford's men were in possession of my spyglass and that even here in the forest my treasured gift was being used upon me. My dear Uncle, I had good reason to start when of a sudden a large deer erupted from the undergrowth beside me and then crashed away between branches only to stop and then turn to watch my own movements with the utmost caution. My heart made a giant leap at this outburst but I felt some assurance that there must be no other human form nearby or I would not have startled the creature so. I then looked down to see that it was a mother's concern that had prevented a full flight, for her new offspring, of perhaps only minutes into this world, lay wet and helpless beside me. I continued on my way, walking

backwards to gain confirmation that the mother would make
a swift return and not now neglect her new born for I would
then be culpable in some fatal disruption of nature. My slow
backwards progress and preoccupation prepared me not one
jot for what happened next. A heavy hand was clamped onto
my pack and the force of this arrest caused the expulsion
of every piece of air from within my chest. This shock and
suspension of breath ended with my choking and gasping for
air which then caused my assailant to hiss and to shake me
violently until I was again silent. Fearing for my life should
I make even the smallest of sounds I slowly turned my head
to find that I was being held at arms length by a man whose
intent lay not upon me for his gaze was directed at the forest
floor. His appearance shocked me as much as the manner
of our encounter for his clothing and hat were draped in
dead snakes and I could not at first comprehend what kind
of wicked magic I had stumbled upon. With my silence now
established the man relinquished his iron grip upon me but
hissed again to deter any further interruption to his business.
He slowly crept a short distance along the path before
leaping with an agility that belied his age, holding before him
a thumbstick and with the cleft to the fore he then stabbed
hard at the ground. A loud curse and a glare in my direction
made it known that I was to be blamed for this opportunity
lost and I believe that my puzzled countenance then provoked
this strange fellow to demonstrate his purpose upon me. After
creeping up close enough for me to smell this man's very

snakeness and with two clawed fingers poised before him he made a sharp hawking noise from his throat before stabbing his hand upon my calf with such a jerk that I jumped up into the air. He roared aloud with a burst of cackling laughter at my distress and in doing so displayed one fang fewer than might be found in a snake's head. The man was keen to parade the many dead snakes that hung from his belt and before I had a chance to express a view on the matter we exchanged hats. With my initiation over, our curious partnership then continued along the path, he determining our slow pace and soft tread and me wearing this strange man's hot and fetid hat and without even a stick to defend myself against the deadly serpent. In a pool of sunlight we soon detected our quarry and I awaited its attack by placing myself well behind this expert in snake combat. The creature did not rear up and confront us but instead it sought a fringe of longer grass to conceal itself and I detected a shyness in its manner and I believe that we had disturbed its sunny slumber. The snakecatcher demonstrated both stealth and swiftness of movement in pinning the creature to the ground with his forked stick and he then smeared its head with the heal of his boot. Before adding this lifeless form to his collection he dangled it before my face and I was taken by the rare beauty of its bold markings and the pale blueness across its underbelly. I removed the man's hat from my head and informed him that I was going to continue on my way for I had no desire to participate in his activity and indeed I felt some sadness at the manner of this creature's death. Our brief partnership was now at an end and I was, of a sudden, viewed with great suspicion as if my purpose here within this snake infested wood was being questioned for the first time. His tongue flickered and in an instant the snakecatcher raised his stick and made to strike me upon the head and it was only my own fleetness of foot that prevented the blow. Many more swipes were directed at my poll as this venomous fiend pursued me along the path until youth prevailed and I left the snakecatcher behind me, bent double and breathless. The legacy of this misadventure is that I am now in possession of an old and stinking felt hat with a desiccated snake for a hat band. My own hat now resides in a place called Cranbourn Chace, if Mr John Cary's map of Wiltshire is to be relied upon, and I make a sincere wish that I never see it again. Upon fleeing from the swinging blows of that woodland devil, whose mind had surely become poisoned by his occupation, I then became hopelessly lost. I hastily cut myself a thumbstick from an azel bush and although it is misshapen and crude and displays no barley twist this pedestrian tourist now feels complete again. It was with no small relief that I eventually left the large and brooding forest behind me and I found a single tree upon a hill and in its shade I succumbed to grateful sleep. I did not wake until shadows began to lengthen and if it had not been for the buzzing flies around my head I may be there still. In a hot daze I stumbled across open downland until I met with the turnpike and there I took directions to the Woodyates Inn.

It has indeed been a very strange day for I have suffered
the important loss of my spyglass, lost and also gained a
hat, retrieved a love letter and also met with an interesting
acquaintance at the Woodyates Inn. Perhaps it was the
day's exposure to a violent sun but as I made my weary way
towards the Inn, there before me in the shimmering heat,
I believed I saw "The Sorrowful Knight" and his "Squire"
approaching upon their trusty steeds. You will know that
these are characters from Cervantes' great novel Don Quixote
and they exist only upon the page where they wander the
Spanish Plains and should not at all be here at the Wiltshire
and Dorset border.

Sir, my candle gutters and will very soon expire along with
your patience and so I must bid you goodnight. I shall now
continue the account of my arrival at the Woodyates Inn
before breakfast.

Your tired and tiresome nephew
HENRY CHALK

Old Wardour Castle

*Mr. Henry Shorto's Cutlery Shop,
Queen Street, Salisbury*

The Doomed Salisbury Canal

MY DEAR UNCLE,

I am sitting before the open window of my room at the mustering of the day and I can report that a Doctor has been summoned for a guest has been taken ill in the night. I make a sincere wish that all will be well yet I hold a palpable fear in the pit of my stomach. There is little that I can do as I await the arrival of the medic, for I cannot sleep, but I may at least recount to you the events of yesterday evening and my arrival at this place. I must also remind myself that it is now early upon Sunday morning for I am much confused by all this disruption. We are, in normal circumstances, still deep in our slumbers at this hour and indeed it is a secret time that only exists in these early summer months. The cockerel has stirred but he has for competition a growing chorus of birdsong that I have not before witnessed and indeed I shall hold still my pen for a moment for when again will this opportunity present itself? My stillness shall be a prayer to my ailing neighbour and I shall close my senses to all but the glorious tribute that heralds the new day.

*

On my approach to the Woodyates Inn I gauged that my arrival would be coincident with that of two figures on horseback and

I had time to muse over the appearance of these characters. I have indicated that I was reminded of those two great inventions of Cervantes: Don Quixote and Sancho Panza and in the early evening sun my fancy exchanged these two unknown travellers for the Noble Knight of the Sorrowful face and his faithful Squire. As the distance between us lessened I could detect that one was of a fuller, rounder shape on a larger horse and the other a taller rider in the saddle but his steed was squat and encumbered with plenty of baggage. Here was surely a reversal of the original arrangement and I afforded myself some simple amusement over this observation. This was after all no parched Spanish plain and I could see no evidence of lance, shield, sword or armour to confirm my idle dreaming and I expected no chivalrous deed. Our arrival at the gateway to the Inn was indeed as I predicted and I raised the snakecatcher's hat, for in the beating sun it was better than no hat at all, and I wished the two Gentlemen the very best of evenings. I could detect no Iberian flavour in a response yet the greeting was both warm and sincere. I introduced myself and the red faced gentleman on the tall horse smiled under a large moustache; "Ah, a fellow adventurer, is not ours the only means of travel? To be enclosed in a wheeled box is to admit to time wasted between destinations, yet we have discovered that all is destination. Let it be our secret, Mr Boyle at your service, my valet Thomas."

Thomas had already found his way to the mounting block and was soon leading the baggage laden animal to the trough where it was left to drink its fill. Mr Boyle then took some prising from his mount by his valet and was even assisted on his descent from the block, demonstrating great stiffness after his time in the saddle. "Do not get old Mr Chalk... or corpulent" called out Mr Boyle across the courtyard, "..for to be both is misery indeed". I drank deeply from the bucket at the well and a stable hand then appeared to attend to the horses and as the master was led into the Inn he loudly voiced his concerns to the valet: "Keep an eye on him Thomas....and see he treats the cavalry well." To which his faithful servant replied with calmness; "I shall return shortly Sir, but I will see you rested first."

I followed behind the weary Knight and his Squire but my way was barred by the landlady who stood with her arms folded for she had evidently witnessed my arrival. "No gent'mun arrives 'pon foot. On yer way."

I had experienced a prejudice before against the pedestrian tourist and with a coating of dust, a hot face and a battered snakecatcher's hat, my appearance did little to endear me to this bony faced woman. I returned to the well to fill my flask and to splash water upon my face and I sat for a while and wondered where I would now pass the night. The valet Thomas returned to observe the stabling of the horses and as I bid him a good evening in passing, he then queried my departure. I explained that pedestrian tourists were a breed that were unwelcome at many establishments and that I had been turned away by the landlady. He remained inscrutable at this news and nodded in return as I again bid him a good evening and then made my way from the courtyard. I had not travelled two hundred yards along the turnpike when I heard a scampering behind me and a calling for me to halt. "Boots" had been dispatched to explain that there had been a misunderstanding and I was after all to be welcomed at the Woodyates Inn. This was indeed a puzzling turnabout of circumstances and on my return I was greeted warmly by the landlord who then cursed his wife's poor manners and I was referred to as "Sir" when often my age and young looks determine that I am addressed as "Master". A comfortable room awaited me and a jug of hot water was soon to arrive and was "Sir available to discuss the evening's menu?" On descending for dinner I was shown to a decent table where nearby Mr Boyle was already in advance of me and was being waited upon by his own manservant, Thomas.

"Ah good news Thomas, good news, we have splendid company tonight in young Mr Henry Chalk, pedestrian tourist". I bid Mr Boyle a good appetite and the inscrutable Thomas raised an eyebrow in acknowledgement before quarter filling his Master's glass with claret. Mr Boyle held up his vessel in protest "We are at war with France but I do not believe that wine is in short supply, fill it up man, fill it up."

Despite the heat of the evening I began a hearty meal and mused that I should be now settling down for the night under a tree with no food at all if it were not for the intervention of the landlord.

"Are you faring any better Mr Chalk for I am enjoying sharp wine and short measures?" My fellow diner then turned to observe that I was not drinking wine at all with my meal and he questioned whether I was ailing. "Thomas, a glass for Mr Chalk."

Upon the conclusion of my meal I was ordered to pull up a chair and join Mr Boyle as he sniffed suspiciously at half a glass of port "I believe that Thomas would have me die of thirst, so Mr Chalk shall we talk of the weather, which is excruciating by the by, or have you an adventure or two that you might share with an old man?" I then described my journey thus far and Mr Boyle appeared interested in my ramblings and as I have not spoken but a few words since leaving Pembrokeshire I was glad to find my voice again. In turn Mr Boyle informed me of his route of which I can but recall a few towns visited; Winchester, Romsey, Ringwood, Wareham, Dorchester and next Salisbury, before the return to London. It is a journey that this same gentleman first undertook in 1782 and many parts of the British Isles have been visited between times. That he had once been a military man I had little doubt and indeed Thomas the valet had earlier confirmed this fact by suggesting that I should raise my voice "for the Colonel has spent a deal of time beside the field guns in battle". Mr Boyle later asked me whether I had at all considered serving my country and I confessed that I had little knowledge of warfare above the playing of lead soldiers and neither had my family any association with army

or naval matters. My dear Uncle, I think back to the weeks
spent in Pembrokeshire and with my late lamented spyglass
how I observed distant ships before they slipped beyond the
horizon. I have even held childish thoughts about a life at sea
and now hold a great admiration for any who cast themselves
upon the wild ocean for before my time on that rugged coast I
had only before witnessed the activities in the Port of London.
I believed then that all was the loading and unloading of ships
with sailors brawling in taverns and I had not perceived what
went on beyond the sanctuary of the brown sliding waters
of the River Thames. I now hold a vision of two unwieldy
warships engaged in battle upon a harsh and boiling sea and
I believe that it is akin to two bugs fighting upon a bears back
for at any moment he might scratch this irritation with one
gigantic paw. It is a visit in my seventh year to the Port of
London that provokes this comparison for there I witnessed a
dancing bear upon the quayside and I will forever make this
curious association. Perhaps bugs have more sense than to
fight amongst themselves. I did not share these thoughts with
the Colonel but I believe that you know me well enough Sir to
tolerate such idle nonsense.

"Danger will put wit into any man Mr Chalk and will be
the making of many a timid fellow". The Colonel then advised
me against joining the Navy "For their ships are but old and
leaky tubs, yet their admirals will be greatly adored by the
people of this island. Sir I can inform you that I commanded
the defence of Frederick of Prussia's rear but you shall not

hear of me when I die. Mr Chalk I do not wish to become maudlin for I will drink of too much brandy but let me now propose a toast; The travelling life and to Colonel Boyle on his last ride and to young Mr Henry Chalk on his second pedestrian excursion," and we duly raised our glasses. Mr Boyle then produced and fuelled his pipe and between whiff and whiff he surprised me by expressing his admiration for that race of eternal travellers referred to as Gypsies. "They know their horses Sir and I shall judge any man by how he regards his horse, be he any creed..excepting of course the Spanish." The Colonel then stated that although their existence and conditions were often pitiful, the Egyptians are a proud race with their own language but are much maligned for they are blamed for any thieving in the district where they make their camp. I informed Mr Boyle that I had not yet met with such people and I was then urged to do so should the opportunity present itself. "They have grimy faces Mr Chalk but their children grow strong out of doors and do not wither in infancy like our own and they understand the horse like no other. Do you ride Sir?"

I confessed that I did not and I was now reticent to describe my distrust of horses and so I promoted you, My dear Uncle, to the Colonel for I know that you have been a keen horseman in your time. I believe that you once sat me upon your horse outside my home in Southwark when I was but a small child and my Mother then rescued me for I disgraced myself by crying pitifully to be let down.

In time Mr Boyle viewed me with watery eyed disapproval through a vale of smoke of his own making. "You are not drinking Sir, and are slowing me down by example." Despite my own temperance and avoidance of port wine altogether, the Colonel drained enough for both our thirsts and instead of retiring to comfortable chairs to continue our conversation, he soon began to snort and snore aloud at the table. Mr Boyle's valet, with the assistance of the landlord, was soon on hand to escort the Colonel to his bed and as a parting gesture this seasoned traveller waved an arm in the vague direction of our capital city and proclaimed loudly "I ride to London in the morning".

I retired to my room to begin this account and in time then tossed and turned in my bed as sleep evaded me in the discomfort of a warm night. I know not at what hour but I heard voices out in the corridor and movement in the neighbouring room. I entered the landing where I found Mr Boyle's valet, Thomas, in a state of some agitation and he was making a request to the landlord that a doctor should be called for immediately. Once the landlord had departed the valet then informed me that what he had feared had come to pass for the Colonel had been taken gravely ill in the night. Thomas retreated to his master's room and there was little I could do other than return to own my room and I soon heard the stable boy upon his mount clatter from the yard to summon the doctor.

I believe that I have slept a while in my chair for the sun is now clear of the horizon. I left the snakecatchers' hat upon the window ledge overnight and I have just been startled by a large black and white bird that was intent on picking at the dead snake hat band. I flapped at the assailant and the mischievous creature then tugged the hat from the sill and caused it to fall. These are quick and intelligent birds that would, I believe, not resist any morsel of carrion or indeed any defenceless living creature. They have a malign rattle for a song like some witch's chatter and I have observed their predatory nature before and I sincerely hope that this bird's presence is not an ill omen for the ailing Colonel. I am thankful that I can hear horses approaching on the turnpike and I believe that it must be the doctor arriving for some hours have now passed and I have heard little movement from the next room. I shall now retrieve my hat from the yard and wish you good morning.

*

Another exceedingly warm day has now passed and I am again before my open window at the Woodyates Inn for I have not yet continued with my pedestrian excursion. I have opened wide the door to my room to encourage a draught and I am inclined to remove some clothing in an attempt to cool myself and yet that might cause alarm to any who cross the landing.

I must resume my account of this morning for the doctor had duly arrived to attend to Colonel Boyle. Whilst at my breakfast the medic then appeared and any concern for his patient was well concealed for he was able to gulp down as much as could be mustered by the landlord. I asked about the condition of the Colonel to which he shrugged; "I have bled him a pint. He will revive or he will not..more cream?"

On returning to my room I received a knock at the door and upon opening it I found the stern faced valet and at first I feared the worst possible news. I still had not become accustomed to this servants lack of expression for instead he requested that I might attend to the ,Colonel as he had expressed a desire to talk to me. Mr Boyle lay pale and clammy in a large bed and turned meekly as I entered the room. "Ah, the pedestrian tourist, not yet on your travels?" I then stated my concern for his wellbeing and wished for a swift recovery and that he might also sit aboard his horse and enjoy the day. "I fear not. Not today Mr Chalk, or perhaps any other day. This was to be my swan song for I have not been well." He then patted the sheet above the girth of his stomach.

The valet departed at a nod from his master and I was then gestured to sit upon the edge of the bed; "I believe that Thomas has made a vow to Mrs Boyle to ensure my safe return to London. He waters the brandy and thinks that I do not notice for as I get older my brandy gets weaker and the port he thins with inferior wine. He ensures me good company of an evening to prevent the melancholy descending and the seeking of comfort in a bottle. He is a fine valet, the best I ever had.." The Colonel then winced after some internal pain and in a whisper began to relate a song or poem;

"Hey nonny no,

Men are fools that wish to die

Ist not fine to dance and sing

When the bells of death do ring?

Ist not fine to swim in wine

And turn upon the toe

And sing hey nonny no

When the winds blow and the seas flow

Hey nonny no

"Our relationship has been brief Mr Chalk and that saddens me, yet I would offer you this, be both brave and bold in life, for otherwise how will a man know his true worth? Have you a passion Sir?"

I informed the Colonel of my curiosity for flint and its import to our ancient ancestors to which he made a weak demonstration of disapproval. "Puh, flint is that cold hard stuff that litters the ground and plagues the hoof, have you not yet found love Mr Chalk for you have much to learn?"

I then spoke of Miss Sarah Foster and our meeting at Hindon but refrained from describing her blindness. Mr Boyle sank back onto his pillow in palpable relief at this news "Then you must display your love," He advised. I explained that I wished that I could compose beautiful poetry and I thought back to the daughter of Ferne House and her letter from one "Percy Bysshe".

"Poetry is worthy, but is there not a gift that might adorn

your loved one, a locket perhaps? There should be no timidity in the scale of the purchase for there is not a price to be placed upon love. Do it on the advice of an old man and I should then die happy in the knowledge that somewhere love does flourish". With that instruction Mr Boyle patted my hand and closed his eyes. I did not believe him to have expired but I then summoned Thomas who continued his bedside vigil.

I could not depart this place and continue on my way with death in the air and so I resolved to stay another night as necessary. I determined that I should at least see part of the day and so I stepped out into the fierce sun with my snakecatcher's hat to wander the neighbourhood.

There is a confusion of earthworks scattered about the Woodyates Inn and if I can believe my judgement, the Inn itself is positioned upon a Roman road. This is most appropriate for an old building that serves the need of travellers yet I doubt if its longevity can be extended to the time of our Roman masters. It is likely that the use of these superior roads continued well beyond that time and indeed the Roman surveyors and engineers have determined today's route for the road to Blandford appears to run straight for as far as the eye can see. These are uncharted territories upon Mr John Cary's map of Wiltshire and I shall have to invest in a map of the neighbouring county of Dorset if I were to extend my excursion into that county. In the opposing direction the raised form of the Roman road can be clearly seen as it departs from the turnpike and strikes off across the down. I then met

with a large ditch that crossed at right angles the Roman road
and conflicted with all Roman principals for it meandered for
some distance across the down before climbing to meet the
horizon. With the huge vallum upon its southern side it spoke
of gargantuan defence against an approach from the north. I
lay back upon its grassy bank to ponder the origin of these
monuments to organised labour. The construction of Roman
roads can somehow be imagined for upon the small world
of a simple village the great machine of the Roman empire
imposed its thoroughfare that was to change forever the lands
that were so familiar to its inhabitants. Every able person
was demanded to participate in achieving this statement
and now through this small world the traffic and trade of the
empire would pass and indeed history had truly arrived for
Tacitus documents these years where previously no written
record survives. The great wandering ditch has more mystery
attached to it for I have not been able to determine whether
the ditch interrupts the course of the Roman road or whether
the road carves through the ditch for it is a confusing junction.
That the ditch was dug in desperate defence there can be no
doubt and this was no simple delineation of boundaries for it
is indeed a great wall of earth.

In time I resumed my excursion and found more confusion
in a plethora of mounds, long barrows and parallel banks
that made my hot head spin with the unravelling of all this
ancient activity, for I could make little sense of it. I wished
for some inhabitant who had miraculously survived the many

millennia, from that day to this, to appear and explain their intent and circumstance. Yet the raising of mounds and banks and the etching of lines upon the landscape are an accumulation across many centuries and I am certain that these mysteries are not solely our preserve. My ancient guide may describe proudly his own contribution but confess that he was at a loss to know what all those long banks and ditches were about.

Upon a shelf this morning at the Woodyates Inn I spied an ancient broken urn and on enquiring of the landlord I established that those indefatigable antiquarians Sir Richard Colt Hoare and Mr William Cunnington have in the past made their excursions from that place. The urn was a gift to their host after excavations at Oakley Down. I informed the landlord that I had accompanied the Baronet in the opening of barrows upon the hills of his own estate at Stourhead. I then confirmed also that I had met with these same Gentleman and their good friend and fellow antiquary, Mr Richard Fenton near the home of Mr William Cunnington where we travelled to the Ashton Valley in the depths of last winter. I shall submit, my dear Uncle, a portion of a letter once intended for you, that describes that event for it has remained unfinished and therefore unsent amongst my travelling papers*.

The landlord appeared unsurprised by my lofty associations and was as courteous as any host that I have

* Printed to the fore of this volume -- Editor

met with on my travels and he requested that I might extend
his best wishes to Sir Richard Colt Hoare to which I happily
consented. I feel perhaps treacherous when I confess that
I am now at odds with the belief that the opening of each
and every barrow that exists upon the chalk hills of South
Wiltshire and North Dorset also, will indeed illuminate
the lives of our ancient ancestors. Are not these recovered
treasures but the crown jewels of the Kings and Queens of
ancient times? I propose that the answer to many a grand
puzzle lays not in the conspicuous but in the inconspicuous;
the fragments of fashioned flint lying where they fell from
the tool makers lap, the interruptions in the natural soils and
chalk that betray past activity, the broken shards of pottery,
a soil encrusted coin or a rusty belt buckle. These are not
the riches of the past but the comings and goings of ordinary
people, of villages long extinct, of forgotten battles and lost
generations. The story of life and death is scattered all about
the place if one but knew where to start.

My dear Uncle, I sensed that I would receive the worst
possible news upon my return to the Woodyates Inn and I
thus dragged my feet and craved distraction at every
turn. As I at last arrived at the front door to that place
a great commotion ensued from within and I was forced
back out into the yard by none other than Colonel Boyle,
as large as life itself and remonstrating loudly with the
landlord. "No Sir, indeed I shall not pay for laying-a-bed this
morning. Thomas, muster the cavalry". On seeing me, and

before I could express my delight at his recovery, Mr Boyle slapped a large hand upon each of my shoulders and roared in my face; "Mr Chalk, it was but a bad bout of the wind and a royal wind it was too. I feared for the window panes at the grand expulsion but all is now well. All is well." The Colonel then shook my hand vigorously and whilst Thomas the valet was ready to assist his master at the mounting block, I shook his hand also and even detected a faint smile as he wished me a good afternoon. As they departed from the yard the Colonel boomed out "Hey nonny no, Mr Chalk. Hey nonny no," and with a flourish of the hand, in my fancy, the Man from La Mancha and his Squire departed for the Sierra Morena.

There have been no more comings and goings or commotions that I can report and all is now quiet. I sincerely hope that I shall sleep well tonight for it has truly been a long day. I have been directing my thoughts towards poetry and yet I have a gulf of ignorance to cross before I shall commit my true feelings to the page. In Cervantes great book there is a playful style, referred to by Mr Richard Fenton as; "versos de cabo rato" and I have, this evening, constructed my own:

> To walk and walk is point
> You may as well in darkness wan
> If flowing water we cannot sav
> Or find a spreading oak to clam
>
> Our silence will detect a rust

And a view seek our atten

A wind will escourt us with its whist

There is too much to see and men

Tomorrow I shall follow the Roman road to Salisbury for there can be no route more straight or direct than a Roman road. Once there I shall purchase an expression of my love for Miss Sarah Foster and for now I shall spare her my poetic blushes.

Your apoetical Nephew
HENRY CHALK

My dear Uncle,

I have now departed the Woodyates Inn and am set fair upon the Roman road. I cannot keep a smile from my face and I must hastily relate my conversation with the landlord of that place. I thanked him for his welcoming me back to the inn after being denied entry in the first instance to which he replied that they should never turn away a young Earl in any guise. I then dispelled any idea of a noble birth and that I was indeed as I appeared, a pedestrian tourist, yet I have paid and tipped as well as any titled traveller. The man grew pale with confusion and questioned again whether I was not Henry Earl of Euston to which I gave my name and stated that I could not account for this misunderstanding. I then bid the landlord a good morning whilst his bony faced wife scowled behind his back as if she were now vindicated in her original action. For a good few hundred paces I could not fathom these curious circumstances until I again considered the characters of Don Quixote and Sancho Panza. Was not the Knight of the Sorrowful Face always under some misapprehension about even his own identity and certainly that of any imaginary foe that he encountered? Yet I do not believe that it was Don Quixote who has committed a chivalrous deed on my behalf by inventing my nobility, but that it was his faithful Squire, the valet Thomas. It was Thomas that witnessed my departure after being turned away from the inn and I now believe it was he that informed the landlord of my erroneous nobility. The valet had made a vow to Mr Boyle's wife to return her husband safe to London and essential to this plan was good company at dinner and a distraction from the bottle. On seeing his master's evening companion fast disappearing along the turnpike he took swift and ingenious steps to reverse the situation. I am honoured that he considered me a worthy distraction and I shall long remember his blank expression and forever regard him as The Resourceful Valet with the Sorrowful Face. I must now gather up my belongings and make swift progress to Salisbury for I believe Mr Boyle's advice to be valid and born of some experience in affairs of the heart.

*

I am currently paddling my feet in the chill waters of a river that flows through the little village of Tony Stratford and my earlier Roman determination has now faltered in the withering sun. One can but admire the vision of our Roman government in the construction of such a highway and its intended longevity. Rabbit burrows and spoil heaps have enabled a view of the layers of chalk and rounded flint pebbles that have been utilised in its upper layers. The chalk can be won from adjacent ditches but I do not believe the rounded gravel to be a local material. The heavy clay cap that often sits upon the crest of the chalk downs only comprises of nodules of flint and has not the water worn appearance of these pebbles. Therefore the quarrying and transportation of substantial quantities of this bulky gravel has been undertaken by the road builders and I wonder at a possible source and also the distances covered in its haulage. At the very base of the raised causeway is a seam of very large irregular flint nodules packed tightly together and it is altogether a construction that would accommodate the heaviest of today's traffic yet it is largely neglected by all travellers. I wonder that it has not become the main turnpike to Salisbury for the work is already done yet there is but a worn thread of human and animal passage that wanders all about the elevation and into the ditches as bushes and burrows are avoided.

The sheep flock with their fattening lambs nuzzle upon the downs and shift as slowly as the puffs of white cloud in a windless blue sky. I wish for more cloud for it would break the sun's present unseasonable conspiracy of burning my skin these last few days and I can now comprehend why shepherds and ploughmen have nut brown faces. Hedgerows offer occasional relief and now display a cloak of white blossom whilst the verges are thick with a creamy flower and it is as if a master confectioner has been at large in the country with his sweet white icing, drizzling it over wayside bushes and whipping it into the banks and verges to produce a bubbling froth.

On descending into the valley I completed a circuit of the village church of Tony Stratford and I can inform you my dear Uncle that it has almost every South Wiltshire stone in its design. There is a pleasing chequer of flint and freestone upon the tower and a combination of red brick and halved nodules of flint about the walls. A round door arch has been constructed from greensand stone amongst which are small fossil shells and it is altogether a jumble that would please the geologist if not the church antiquarian. To further offend this latter breed I did not enter the building and can therefore offer no critical description of aisle, nave, chancel, plate or rood. The church is placed precariously upon a bank above the river and there has been some considerable buttressing upon the northern walls to prevent the whole from joining the valley floor.

The range of local materials has been ably demonstrated by the creeping church yet two items are missing and one has been rectified by a neighbouring cottage that appears to have solid chalk blocks incorporated into its walls. There must be a seam of chalk hereabouts that can withstand the weather and not crumble at the first visit of Jack Frost and I hope that I shall be able to record further examples. The church has also spurned the use of mud yet it is surely the most available of all materials and I can record that I have witnessed its use here in Tony Stratford with the building of a small house. I believe that it is a simple and ancient ingenuity where a dwelling can be constructed from its immediate surrounds without recourse to the costly excavation and carriage of materials and I shall attempt to describe this process. Upon a tall base of flint nodules a sloppy mix of soil and chalk has been cast by the bucketful, yet to give form to this operation long planking has been shored up at the horizontal to create the eventual thickness of the walls. These are temporary sides that prevent the immediate seepage of this material until it dries and I gauge that the planks are then raised and trussed up against the next level and the process begins anew. This blazing sun causes ideal conditions for the drying to occur and perhaps within only a single day the mix is firm and in this fashion, piece by piece, the solid walls of a simple house will in time be created. Door frames and windows are but simple wooden poles introduced to form the necessary apertures and I suspect that the whole will conclude with a roof of straw. To the side of the building the various components of valley soil, chalk and also small flints have been gathered and thrown together into a congealed wet mess. A small horse has been assigned to trample about this heap as pails of river water are splashed before the hooves of the animal and even the beasts own droppings flop into this unruly mix. My close interest in this whole process has caused some entertainment to the four men and a boy employed to the task. I believe that from my appearance they perceive me to be an itinerant snakecatcher and so in the passing of but two hours I have fallen in my standing from Earl to a lowly hunter of vermin and an object of amusement to a gang of mud splattered labourers. One of these men first pointed to the feet of another under the pretence that there was a serpent about to strike to which the fool would jump about and cry out in mock alarm. They would then all join in with this mirth and begin drawing imaginary snakes from their pockets and from beneath their hats. One poor fellow took fright that such a game would conjure up a living peril so great was his fear of these creatures. With this weakness now displayed he was then fiercely pursued by another and on having a muddy hand thrust down the back of his shirt, he took off in a flapping panic. He then abruptly ceased his flight and shook violently his clothing until he was able to confirm with an expression of simple satisfaction that there was no viper present after all and his life could now continue. I slipped away during this commotion to paddle my feet and eat a crust of bread taken from the table of the Woodyates Inn and also to expend some ink.

*

My dear Uncle, I sincerely hope that my pack and thumbstick are still concealed under a thorn bush where I left them at the outskirts of the city of Salisbury and for ink, paper, pen, nightshirt, supper and a bed I have again the generosity of strangers to thank.

It is another exceedingly warm night and the sounds and odours of this place float up to my open window for I occupy a room at the very top of Mr and Mrs Shorto's house in Rollestone Street. Mr Shorto is an esteemed cutler of the City of Salisbury and metal is at the heart of his business and yet it is the discourse upon the provenance of flint at our initial meeting that has brokered this friendship. I fear, however, that I make a disruptive presence within the home of a kind and respectable family and I shall endeavour to explain this matter in due course. At first light I shall depart and leave behind a cowardly note of apology and I wish that I should heed my own advice in not becoming involved in the lives of others for it always leads to complication.

I must now retrace my steps and turn back the clock to before noon where on a ridge above the City it was finally necessary to depart from the Roman road for to continue on its course would lead me to Sorviodunum, or Old Sarum, when my quest required the services of its sibling, New Sarum. The turnpike brought me in turn to the south of the City with a view of the Cathedral that must surely demand a halt by even the most weary of travellers. Yet I am reminded of Mr Boyle and his detestation of wheeled traffic for I was near run over by a flying stage as it hurtled by in a downhill fury with unstoppable anxiety to appease the clock and to rush its hot and bothered cargo betwixt destinations. As the Spire beckons and guides the traveller toward the City it is first necessary to cross a broad river and to this end a fine stone bridge has been constructed with multiple arches and its antiquity must surely challenge its lofty rival. Upon entering the Close itself and approaching the Cathedral it is only your own tiresome nephew that would become animated by the presence of flint in the exterior wall of the cloister upon the southern side. It is a rear view that I am certain is not presented for general inspection for it has a rough appearance comprising of irregular stone and successive courses of flint. It is a feature that most tourists to Salisbury would not notice far less comment upon even as an unsightly comparison to the grandeur of the stonework and carvings upon the western end. I, however, felt gratified that the simple utility of flint has found a place in surely one of the finest buildings in the whole world. I believe that I have promised before to offer a full account of Salisbury Cathedral but I fear that it shall not be today. Upon leaving the Close and entering the tangle of humanity that occupies the streets of Salisbury I was made to question the wisdom of my excursion to the City for my nose soon longed for a gust of fresh air but encountered none. I later questioned my host, Mr Henry Shorto, about the plethora of rivulets and gutters that accompany each and every street in this place. As a visitor I did not wish to quickly find fault but there is a stench where certain of these drains accumulate filth and where men with long poles and rakes are employed to assist the passage of this detritus and yet there are other sections that flow with more certainty. There is a daily cleansing of the accumulations of the nightly chamber pot caused by the opening of up stream hatches where fresh water is diverted from the River Avon through this street system and the foul is flushed back downstream into the parent river. Mr Shorto informed me with a laugh that Salisbury has been referred to as the "English Venice" with its streams and little culverts and bridges and yet it is with a serious tone that he then warned of this open system through the hotter months and its association with flies and a mortal sickness that has claimed a great many residents. This clawing at the back of my throat hastened my purpose for I have lived away from the City long enough to forget its pernicious flavours and I quickly scoured the shop fronts for some meaningful gift yet I knew not what I was searching for. I soon found myself in the market square which today was not gathered but tomorrow is I believe market day and this place will become busier still.

I am a poor reporter of topography and even less so of civic affairs yet there is a new Council House built in one corner of the square that is very grand and shouts of pride and prosperity should there be any doubt on that score. There are also a great many streets at right angles to each other in the City which suggest an orderly plan yet the buildings themselves are too haphazard and irregular in form for the eye to consider it a place of real beauty. But what do I know my dear Uncle for there are many better qualified to pass such a judgement rather than this simple pedestrian tourist?

It was whilst I stood pondering my purpose in this place that I believe I witnessed one of my own species pass by, for a pedestrian tourist in a busy city street is a conspicuous creature indeed. I have, for the sake of anonymity, temporarily shed my own accoutrements as I did not wish to become prey to any rogue or pickpocket as happened on my first visit to Salisbury. This fellow had a full pack and sturdy boots and tapped at the city streets with his thumbstick with all the while an expression of bemused curiosity upon his face.

He holds our secret in his breast for he knows that once he leaves behind the people of Salisbury to their prosaic tasks then adventure and the unknown lie just around the corner. There must be a map about his person and perhaps a book that has inspired this excursion and I wonder also if there is somewhere an exasperated recipient for the prolific correspondence engendered by each fresh experience. I wished to approach and have my questions answered yet I believe that we are not a breed that would naturally flock together but are a more solitary animal. To gather in a herd would be to amplify the tread upon a path and alert every bird and beast of our presence and these treasured encounters may therefore be lost. I had stalked my prey along two sides of the market square before I realised that I was doing so until, in Queen Street, I ceased my pursuit and let this furtive gentleman slip from my view for he then turned a corner and was gone. I then felt a great urge to depart from the city and return to my own adventure and yet I had still my quest to fulfil. Across the street, having been led to this spot by my quarry, my attention was then drawn to a curious sign above a shop for it was a large folding knife that on a much smaller scale would be intended for the pocket and yet this object would ably serve a giant. I investigated further and found this to be a cutler's shop and the proprietor was one Mr Henry Shorto. The window displayed a fine and overwhelming range of goods with silverware and jewellery also promoted and yet it was the wording upon a small card that arrested my eye for it stated simply; "Gunflints". This was encouragement enough and I entered the shop but soon found myself in near total darkness for my eyes could not easily adjust to the gloomy interior by contrast to the sun's brilliance out in the street. After blinking and rubbing my eyes I soon regained my vision and found before me a young couple who were obviously much in love and I dared to imagine Sarah and myself one day being so bold together in a public place. That they were married I held no doubt for the lady had selected a silver locket and the husband then took great care in fastening the chain clasp from behind as the lady held up her hair to enable access for this delicate operation. I wished to observe the success of this possible purchase but with discretion and so I feigned to study some nearby silver gravy boats and indeed my interest was perceived as genuine by one of the shop assistants. He then described in detail the merits of one gravy boat upon another and I now know all that is to be known regarding silver gravy boats and narrowly resisted embarking upon a final transaction to alleviate the awkwardness of the situation. That my poor Sarah should become the bewildered recipient of such a curious gift was unthinkable and I only had to imagine Mr Boyle's exasperation at such foolishness; "A gravy boat Mr Chalk. You travelled to Salisbury with your love in mind and purchased… a gravy boat?"

I left the gravy boats and lamented that I had been unsuccessful in my observation of the trial of the silver locket and I instead retreated to the rear of the shop. The same assistant came in polite pursuit of his customer who was evidently hard to please and had now drifted from silver gravy boats to powder flasks and dog whistles. I then expressed my interest in gunflints to the tireless employee who asked "what sort of gun does Sir possess?" To which I responded that I had no kind of firearm but wished to observe gunflints nevertheless. The man obliged and set out a number of different sized gunflints upon a counter and politely left me for a more reasonable customer. These flints were neatly trimmed and of a dark and fine quality stone for there were no flaws, flecks or any irregularities and it was of a superior quality to that from Peter Winter's pit in Grovelly Wood where I had last year joined him in his work. Of a sudden a voice stirred me from my concentration upon these dark flint nuggets. "I have been informed that you wish to view gunflints and yet do not possess a gun. They are indeed the least expensive items in the shop and I am intrigued that you find them the most interesting." I looked up to find a Gentleman of perhaps thirty years, dressed smartly but with the sobriety of a businessman. He introduced himself as the owner of the establishment "Mr Henry Shorto at your service and if you will pardon my impertinence, that is a very curious hat that you are wearing Sir, for I have not before witnessed an adder upon the premises, albeit a dead one." I in turn introduced myself and yet I did not at first accept Mr Shorto's interest as sincere but I was soon to realise my failing. I explained that my hat was acquired whilst going about my business as a pedestrian tourist and such things were to be expected. Mr Shorto had a kindly face and was not to be easily dissuaded from engaging in conversation despite my ill tempered awkwardness. "Indeed? I sometimes crave adventure..and yet I have a business and family to attend to." Mr Shorto then picked up the largest of the gunflints and turned it around thoughtfully in the grip of finger and thumb "I am told that they rarely fail but then I do not possess a gun..I believe that I would gain little pleasure from fowling and would sooner study Mr Bewick's illustrations than put to death a woodcock or a shoveller duck. So what is it Mr Chalk, this mysterious substance we call flint for I can admit to some degree of fascination myself regarding its provenance although I have never, before today, confided in another upon the matter? Do you hold a view?"

I soon found something endearing in Mr Shorto's manner and I informed him of the progress of my own interest and understanding and the good fortune of my encounters with those tireless antiquarians Sir Richard Colt Hoare of Stourhead and Mr William Cunnington of Heytesbury. Indeed it was the latter Gentleman that recently wrote to me on this self same matter and I was able to quote verbatim his ever sensible and balanced views to Mr Shorto. The natural provenance of flint has long been a subject of speculation and there are three schools that vie for the trophy of breaking this mystery. It is the glassiness of flint that first promoted the idea that it must be formed by heat and a state of fusion in the manner that glass is so formed and it was therefore an igneous business. Another way is that flint was once soluble and has solidified from an aqueous mass and this may account for the curious bulbous shaping of the nodules and so the chemists might win with this notion. The third way belongs to the biologists and that flint is in someway due to the marine animals and indeed they have left their clue as fossils within the chalk.

A boy of perhaps twelve years wearing a long apron appeared from a room at the rear of the shop and waited politely until he had gained the proprietors attention but remained unnoticed as Mr Shorto thought at length about these three possibilities.

"So which is it to be Mr Chalk; igneous, chemical or biological for I should dearly like to know?" The boy looked up at me as if he also wished for clarification to a problem that had so apparently vexed his Master. I confessed that it required a scientific mind to resolve these issues and ignorance on the subject prevented me from throwing my hat into the ring. Mr Shorto smiled and then stooped to attend to the needs of the young employee who having now gained his instruction departed quickly from whence he came. I felt that I could take this Gentleman into my confidence regarding my true purpose in his shop and Mr Shorto listened attentively before making his own suggestions. He then guided me to the jewellery cases and demonstrated great patience as we handled the finest silver and gold items and discussed the merits of each and every one. Despite this good progress we strayed again to the mystery of flint for we both found it an easy diversion and instead of fine filigree and Welsh gold our subjects became fossils and fashioned flint. Mr Shorto then drew out his watch and stated that he must now cross the street to the workshop and requested that I might like to join him and that we could continue our discussion on the way with a promise that we should soon return to fulfil my quest. I readily agreed and was introduced to the business of cutlery from the sulphurous odours, immense heat and ear splitting noise of the forge to the busy fingers of the improvers in the workshop. I had not before regarded iron and steel as being of any consequence as they are so bound up in modern enterprise and industry that I have shied away from such matters. I confessed my ignorance to Mr Shorto who suggested that the creation of metal from rock was of an equal significance to mankind as perhaps the creation of fire from flint and the fashioning of flint tools. I observed the bladesmith at his work with new interest as if he now of a sudden represented the many ancient metalworkers that have over centuries crafted daggers, swords and other weaponry before a blinding heat. My eyes were drawn inexorably to this small but fiercely white hot fire within the hearth that provided the means to treat and form the metal whilst a man at the bellows kept a steady breath of oxygen to feed and regulate this conflagration. Another man was on hand to grip with iron tongs these brilliant bands of red metal, drawing them swiftly from the hearth before slamming them upon the anvil and striking down mightily with a bouncing hammer blow to shed sparks and make my ears ring for this operation is repeated many times over. There were others hearths around which more workers concentrated their efforts and where these glowing strips were then quenched in a water butt to hiss and steam for a very short while before examination and further plunging. In one dark corner a worker at a treddle grinding wheel then screamed a shower of sparks against the wall of the forge as a blade was shaped and Mr Shorto tugged at my sleeve to indicate that we should depart and once in the street conversation again became a possibility. His was not the only forge for there were others nearby and the chimes of this anvil music could be heard resounding around this quarter to which my guide referred to as the Coal Market. I questioned Mr Shorto on the stage of blade production that I had witnessed and it appears as though a piece of steel could be placed between two sections of wrought iron and then be fiercely heated and hammered until it became a single piece of metal. This is a process called "Mooding" and ensures the sharpness and longevity of the cutting edge. The quenching of hot strips in a butt of water is a means to "Temper" or harden the metal and the time in the water is critical for the cooling metal can display a veritable rainbow of colours each indicating a differing eventual property to the blade. Mr Shorto confirmed that this judgement by the Quencher was born from long experience and upon this great skill the reputation of the Salisbury cutlery trade depended more than any other. A knife may appear fine with its handle ornamented in gold but it would only ever be as good as its blade.

We then ducked into a doorway in the Butcher Row which by contrast appeared a world away from the hellish forge and yet it was here that the various blades were introduced to handles, hinges and springs and all the various components that made up the finished articles. Broad windows ensured that a half dozen quick fingered craftsmen standing before benches could locate rivets and punches and Pearlers could file and embellish their fine work whilst each had a small vice to hold steady their task. In this way folding knives and scissors, carving knives and cutlery for the table, all of the finest quality are made, and upon each is present the stamp of **SHORTO SARUM.**

My Dear Uncle my wrist is cramped by the task of writing and I have no other to blame but myself. I wish to complete my account and yet I must put down this pen, I do not believe that I shall disturb the bed that has been made available to me and I shall instead study a while Mr Bewick's book of birds that belongs to my kind host.

I know not what hour it is but I do not yet sense a lightening of the sky beyond the open curtains. I have been contemplating why I should feel obliged to commit so much to the page and not to just let events pass by without record. I fear that it might be that I only exist upon the page and ink is therefore my life blood. I have not again met with Sarah from the time of our first chance encounter at Hindon and as a consequence all has since been conducted through the pen. If I ceased to write to my love then I should then cease to be, for the more alive I feel the more I shall write and I do feel alive whilst at large in South Wiltshire. Until Robert Foster returns home I cannot communicate with his sister but I fear Sir that I must live through my correspondence to you. I do sincerely apologise for the size of my handwriting and I am certain that it must cause you great exercise for the eye but as the cost of postage increases by the page it is indeed a matter of economy. I believe that you will say "Spare the cost, my persistent Nephew, spare your wrist and therefore spare my eyes."

As you will know by now, I am a guest at the home of Mr and Mrs Shorto, for a swift invitation transpired when I suggested to my host in his shop, once we had established the nature of my gift to Sarah, that I must now depart from the City and continue my journey. Mr Shorto was most insistent that I should do no such thing and that I must spend the night under his roof for we still had much to discuss. I was introduced to Mrs Eliza Shorto and their very young family and indeed Mrs Shorto has not long been out of confinement and I heard from the nursery Master Edward Shorto exercising his lungs to great effect. Mrs Shorto was very welcoming and interested to hear of my family and circumstances and as dinner progressed she then established that both my parents were deceased and that I had no other relation other than you Sir, my Uncle. Mr Shorto attempted to guide the conversation to other territories and yet Mrs Shorto wished to establish why I was not then in Southwark at Chalk's brewery to attend to my duties there and to oversee my Father's business. Her husband had indeed found himself in the self same position after the tragic loss of first his Mother Ann who died in childbirth and then six years later his Stepmother Elizabeth also lost in childbirth followed by his Father Henry, who died of a broken heart the very next day. I offered my surprise and sincere commiserations at this news but I had not yet heard the concluding moral to this tale for the cutlery business was then carried on by Mr Henry Shorto, at the age of eighteen, "For the sake of the family."

Her husband cleared his throat and offered a toast at this disclosure;

"To Sarum . . .

The height of its steeple,

The pride of its people,

It's scissors and knives,

And diligent wives"

At the conclusion of our meal Mrs Shorto, although pale in countenance, had sufficient energy to demonstrate her skill upon an instrument called a guitar. It was apparently made in Salisbury by one Benjamin Banks who was largely renowned for the construction of violins and they are indeed favoured by the best musicians in England and I was instructed that Salisbury had not only to be justly proud of its cutlers but of its musical instruments also. The nine strings of the guitar were gently plucked to accompany a delicate voice as her husband and I sat attentively in the drawing room whilst Mrs Shorto treated us to her full repertoire. Fatigue, I believe, curtailed the performance to a premature end to which she apologised whilst we applauded and as Mrs Shorto retired, we then rose to bid her a goodnight and retreated to Mr Shorto's study. The business of flint was quick to surface and I explained that whilst my current quest was to locate a source of quality flint, I had also a fanciful notion to one day publish a short volume entitled; "Manufactured flint tools and their essential use in everyday life before the common availability of metal by the ancient people of South Wiltshire." Mr Shorto thought this an excellent idea and then suggested that he might prosecute his own investigation into the origin of flint and would read every known fact on the matter and to explore himself any available outcrop of native flint to assist in solving this conundrum. We then made a toast to seal this pledge and Mr Shorto proposed that my work should perhaps be entitled "Life before the knife and fork" whereupon I raised a glass to my host and to his investigations into "Undergroundology". Once we had mocked each other's venture I made an earnest enquiry to establish the source of iron and steel that was so crucial to the business of cutlery for one day I should like to witness the creation of crude iron from rock. Mr Shorto stated that he believed his early predecessors had long depended upon a supply of bar iron from the New Forest in Hampshire and indeed foundries and the smelting of iron continues there to this day and they largely fulfil a naval requirement. A variety of domestic sources now supply Salisbury's Cutlery production and even the raw material, iron ore itself, is shipped about the place as from a variety regions they offer differing properties and their utility is quite specific. As an example Mr Shorto cited grey ore as being very suitable for the production of gun metal and the craft of barrelmaking is long established within the City. In addition the mechanised, and as a consequence "inferior", Sheffield cutlery industries imported a large proportion of bar iron from Sweden. My host explained that Salisbury had suffered very recently in its ability to import and export goods by canal, which is a system that so ably supports the Northern cutlery industries. The Salisbury canal is now bankrupt and falling into neglect and Mr Shorto considered it a tragedy for it was never concluded at its approach to Salisbury and the City had still to depend on wheeled transport to supply its every need. I enquired as to the location of the canal for I may now inspect this fated project as it will guide me to a quarter of the County of Wiltshire that I have not yet visited. Mr Shorto lamented that he should dearly wish to accompany me but his duties would not permit this yet it was hoped that perhaps in the future the business of cutlery may excuse his absence for a short while and he might himself become a pedestrian tourist. Mr Shorto also signalled that he held a perpetual dread as to the health of his wife and young family and I have already described the open channels to which my host addresses the cause of the exceptional mortality in this

City especially in the warmer months. I was greatly shocked
to learn that Mr Shorto lost five brothers and sisters in infancy
and I wonder that there should be a cure sought to expunge
Salisbury's fatal epithet of "Little Venice". I understood fully
why my host was reluctant to leave his home and family for
any period beyond his working hours.

Mr Shorto has promised to forward my gift for Sarah to
the Winterslow Hut where, you will recall, I have arranged
to meet with her brother Robert Foster. My host then kindly
provided the means to make this correspondence and he
escorted me to my room. I thanked him warmly and revealed
that I now considered him a true friend to which he responded
that he owed me much for making a fire under the question of
the origin of flint where only a spark had existed before. "We
shall resume over breakfast, goodnight Henry." That I have
blown into the lives of these good people like some strange
and disorientated foreign bird can surely only disturb and
raise a dormant curiosity of life beyond the City boundary. In
my heart I knew that as my friend greeted the new day then
I would have already departed Salisbury's choking confines
and shall again be reunited with all the accoutrements of the
pedestrian tourist.

Your irresponsible nephew
HENRY CHALK.

MY DEAR UNCLE,

I cannot pretend Sir for I feel weary and lacking in sleep these last few days and today has already signalled its intent for it is still early and I can already sense a building heat. I have again found a river beside which to rest a while and there is much to observe as it slips by. A fly presses down its long legs upon the water skin whilst a shadowy predator below noses up against the surface and it is as if this tense barrier between these two worlds can never be broken. With a muscular flop, the water is shattered, the fly eaten and the fish returns to its lair to digest its prey. Perfect rings grow and fade toward the bank and the sky's reflection is once more restored and another fly settles. I believe that I could sit and watch this sequence over and again and the poor fly can find no sanctuary either whilst in lazy flight for a small brown fan tailed bird will dart from a bush upon the bank to snap up this morsel in one blink of my eye. This fly has been dealt a poor hand and must question its purpose upon this earth between snap and snap if it has the time, or more crucially, the wit to do so.

Mr Boyle determined that I should be brave and bold in life and yet I quietly slipped the latch at Mr and Mrs Shorto's house at the first cock crow leaving behind me a cowardly note.

I believe that my spirit of adventure has had an unsettling effect upon that household for responsibility is graded above gratuitous wandering by Mrs Shorto and I believe Sir that it is a sentiment to which you may wholly concur. I will, in time, correspond with Mr Shorto for he has confided in me that whilst cutlery is his trade it is not his passion and that place shall be reserved for his future study into the origin of flint.

My being on the streets in the early morning enabled me to again experience the accumulations within the drainage channels for the hatches had not yet been opened to flush away these human and animal suppurations. Today is market day in Salisbury and upon the approaching streets I met with the mustering of beasts with their attendant masters. A dairy cart clattered by to join the growing throng and I bought a penny loaf from a baker boy's basket. I thought to fill my flask from a pump but shied from the Salisbury water least it should be privy tainted and chose instead to wait until I reached a neighbouring village. Beside the Close wall I saw a family of small water birds dipping and diving under these still and opaque waters and even the young and paler offspring were practising this dipping for food. At my approach the family squeaked in alarm and found sanctuary under the bridge before the eastern gate to the Cathedral grounds and I believe that the channel emanating from these Holy quarters held no less a stench from that of the remainder of the City.

My belongings remained undisturbed beneath their thorny lodging and once reunited I then followed a drover's road to

the village of Britford. At that place I took directions to the
ferry for it was a route proposed by my host, Mr Henry Shorto
and I was required to cross broad and lush meadow land and
I was there able to witness a system of ditches and raised
channels controlled by wooden hatches. I believe that it is
a complex means by which to irrigate the grass that I do not
fully understand but that sheep have been grazing freely here
I hold no doubt. Across the river there is a small boat moored
and a ferryman's cottage where I have observed a woman at
her washing but she has not yet spied me. She is indeed the
ferrywoman for two women with baskets brimming with posies
now require passage across this broad river and I shall hastily
collect myself and make an opposing journey.

*

I have earned my crust as a diligent pedestrian tourist for
I have endured the direct sun in prosecuting a drawing of the
canal. Mr Shorto informed that it was now abandoned and
laid to waste and yet I have witnessed activity of sufficient
interest to find employment for my pencil. A great volume of
chalk has been extracted from pits adjacent to the canal and
deposited in a barge for transportation to a farm some ten
miles east of this village of East Grimstead. The small church
in the drawing now offers me some sanctuary from the rays
of the sun and if I may intrude upon your time once more I
shall relate my progress thus far for it is not without interest.
At the ferry, once the two market bound passengers with their
baskets of fresh posies were deposited upon the bank, I was

fully prepared to step aboard the craft and make my crossing. The ferrywoman however held a different view and instead, with a few stiff pushes upon the pole, returned immediately to the opposite mooring and despite my protestations stepped ashore without so much as a glance in my direction. It was as if I did not exist and perhaps in her world, of the passing and the repassing of familiar faces, I did not. I had no option but to pull off my boots and string them around my neck, remove my stockings, lift up my coattails and step into the oozy bankside mud. The passage underfoot was stony and I prodded ahead of me with my thumbstick. At its deepest the water rose to cover my breeches and I fancied that the river was tainted with the smell of the Salisbury drainage channels for it is indeed the receptacle for this filth. After hauling myself from the river I wished to glower at the ferrywoman to show that my progress had not been affected by her obstructive nature yet she was nowhere to be seen. I soon encountered more passengers who viewed me with great circumspection as it was obvious by my dripping condition that I had passed through the river and not over it. I raised the snakecatcher's hat and wished an elderly couple a good morning and trusted that they would be met with more civility than I had just been dealt with by the ferrywoman. The couple chose not to respond and instead scuttled by as if I were some blackguard and I felt certain that their tongues would soon be engaged in exchanging suspicions with the ferrywoman. I continued on my way whistling as loudly as I was able to demonstrate to this closed corner of Wiltshire that I cared not one jot for their welcome. In time I replaced my stockings and boots and made steady uphill progress away from the broad and flat plain of grass meadows and mused that the river was now pushed up tight against this valley cliff. In distant times the entire valley, some miles wide, must have been scoured by a vast and swollen mass of destructive water and yet today it was a mere trickle by this comparison. I should like to see the ferrywoman navigate the ancient course of this river for she would require a pole of perhaps one hundred feet in length.

The land about soon displayed signs of a change in the soil, with orange sand spilling out of rabbit burrows and with a concentration of the oak tree which does not seem to prosper so well upon the chalk. As the road continued its upward curve I noticed where gravel pits had been recently dug on a broad verge and I believe their purpose is to service the road itself. That gravel existed here was of interest enough to one who is so easily pleased by even the mildest geological occurrence and yet as the road straightened a most peculiar and unsettling sight unfolded before me. Huddled amongst a continuation of these pits were clusters of men in grimy yellow uniforms with red waistcoats and they had evidently spent the night here for the smoke from dampened fires hung heavily in the air. Standing in groups upon the road were militiamen with muskets and with a further number preparing to mount their horses I had little doubt that the men amongst the gravel pits were prisoners and the whole party was about

to depart from this makeshift camp. I drew close enough
to hear a drift of conversation amongst the seated men to
establish that these were indeed French prisoners of war in
transit. I could see now that these were not English faces and
yet they were unhealthily pale with too much of the shape
of the skull showing through stretched skin and as I passed
I was made to feel greatly ill at ease by their hollow eyes
as they followed my progress. One prisoner hissed to gain
my attention and the nearest militiaman, of perhaps my own
age, waved the barrel of his musket up to the horizontal to
indicate for the Frenchman to remain silent. The prisoner
however persisted and revealed a small white figure, perhaps
carved from bone, and then rubbed his thumb and forefinger
together and whispered hoarsely "Moneys, moneys". The
young militiaman advanced and gave the man a firm prod
with the barrel of his gun and called for silence "Else I'll send
you back to the stinkin' 'ulks see if I wont". The emaciated
prisoner then retreated to the smoky shadows of the gravel
pit to crouch down amongst his fellow captives. I asked
the soldier what was to be the destination for these men to
which he looked first at my battered snakecatcher's hat and
then at the shiny wetness of my breeches before stating that
it was no concern of mine and indicated with a jerk of his
head for me to be on my way. The whole party was evidently
waiting on the arrival of the Captain and as I left behind
me the prisoners and their escort, the mounted Captain and
two officers appeared from their nights lodging at the Green

Dragon Inn. In France I judge that there must be a reversal of this situation with English prisoners of war held captive and how many hundreds, thousands or indeed perhaps many thousands of men? I have been sheltered from the bare facts of war as English life continues; dairymaids are abroad in the early morn, beasts are herded to market, cutlery is produced, barrows are dug by noblemen and yet war goes on beyond the horizon. My ears cannot hear the crack and shriek of battle and yet today my eyes have surveyed the emaciated ghosts of free men and as I ambled through the village of Alderbury it was if I were troubled by an unsettling dream. Dreams must turn to vapour with the reassurance of the morning sun and yet inside I feel a scratch upon my soul for this very morning I have witnessed another's nightmare.

*

My soul has received a greater laceration and my conscience is greatly troubled. I wish for guidance but I am alone. I do not feel that I have the spirit to continue with my account and yet I must somehow unburden myself. Would that you were here beside me, my dear Uncle, for you remain the last attachment to my family and I have foolishly closed my eyes to summon your presence. Sir, I have drunk brandy with no evening meal and the candles waver so

My stomach is now truly empty and I have revived my sorry condition by placing my head under the courtyard pump of this place and it is a place that I do not even know the name of other than it is an Inn upon the road to Romsey.

My biliousness will pass and I should screw up this nonsensical page and start anew for it smells of bile. Please forgive me.

I have a sorry tale of my own treachery to tell and if the fug in my head will permit it, I shall begin and yet I cannot even recall where I left myself without casting my eye back over the page. Indeed it was the small church beside the canal where I hid from the cruel sun to take up my pen and write to you and then slept a while. I could not readily awaken from this slumber amongst the graves and for a time I wobbled along the tow path rubbing my eyes and yawning at the bankside creatures as they fled my heavy footfall. At the next lock I met with the cargo of chalk that had since departed from the bridge and I wondered whether the levels of water in the canal were sufficient to float this heavily laden vessel. The four hauling men were already perspiring from their labour upon the rope and were now required to begin again as they aligned themselves on the towpath. From my earlier enquiry I had established that the two men upon the barge were the barge owner, who had brought the vessel up from Lockerley and the farmer who had purchased the chalk as a manure to enrich his fields. The barge haulers from West Dean had been engaged to dig and load the chalk from the pit and must be grateful for this employment for as Mr Henry Shorto had indicated the canal was now bankrupt and with no prospect of a future. Upon the still surface of the canal a bright green carpet of small leafed weed has been able to accumulate on these undisturbed waters and I wondered at the effects of future neglect. To enable passage even for local requirements water levels must be managed correctly and locks maintained and I reflected that I had perhaps witnessed one of the last voyages upon this doomed canal. I bid the company farewell and slow pedestrianism soon left the barge and its gleaming cargo well behind.

Before the village of West Dean an inconvenient spur of land has presented a great obstacle to the steady progress of the canal and a deep cutting has been made. I wonder that the planned route did not deviate to avoid this undertaking and follow instead the course of its living ancestor that naturally makes it own easy passage around the hill. Water will find its own route but to engineer its course, a succession of locks must be constructed to assist with this artifice whilst here a whole hillside has been gouged out and piled high upon steep banks. I scrambled to the summit of the grassy slope and was gratified to discover the necessity for this great excavation as the façade of a large and very grand house soon revealed itself with its many windows having a southern aspect. The owner has therefore not welcomed the view of the canal with its passage of chalk, coal, timber or any other commodity nor witness the honest toil and language of the barge haulers.

After this polite and enormously costly diversion the canal and river converge at West Dean and surely it is a village that believed that it should prosper from this bold enterprise with its broad wharf, warehouse and Inn. It is as if the cast of this busy drama had deserted the stage to leave behind the set and scenery and indeed the theatre had been abandoned save for myself in the open auditorium and one soul who had made his bed upon a heap of horse dung in one corner of the yard beside the inn. His contribution in this production is to snore loudly and he embraces his part with gusto. Lo! Enter stage left a phaeton drawn by a single horse, imagine the clip clop if you will, and aboard is I believe a Parson. The horse is led to drink on this hot day and the Parson surveys the scene and spies the man asleep upon the dung heap. He calls across; "You there, you there". There is no response from the dung heap except perhaps that the snoring gets louder. The Parson repeats his lines "You there, you there". The horse is left to drink its fill and the parson climbs down from the phaeton and strides across the yard and stops before the dung heap; "You there..." You will by now have gauged that this is not Shakespeare, Sheridan nor even Kelly, but the work of an undiscovered talent, Henry Chalk, and I believe that it is the brandy that has skewed my senses but continue I must. Back at the dung heap the Parson's wrath at this dissolute behaviour has caused him to poke the snoring man with his stick to which, in response, there is a change of pitch but not of volume. The Parson steps gingerly upon the foothills of the dung heap and then grips the coat of this resolute sleeper and tugs with all his Christian might. The snores are replaced by a puzzled grunting and this disturbance is resolved by the shrugging free of the troublesome coat by the disturbed fellow who then crawls back to the comfortable summit of the dung heap. The Parson meanwhile is dusting off his breeches for he flew off in the opposing direction along with the empty garment. The coat is then cast to ground and an assault made upon the steaming mount, the soundly sleeping man is dragged by the ankles and he drowsily tries to gain purchase with outstretched arms to arrest this downward motion and succeeds only in removing two handfuls of dung from the pile. Having now achieved his primary goal the Parson hauls the man to the vertical and embarks upon a sermon on the pernicious evils of drink. The sleeper sways gently for a moment before pressing a handful of dung into the face of his assailant and then turns and clambers back upon the soft and odorous pile and the snoring resumes.

At this juncture I came to the aid of the clergyman for he was blinded temporarily and he rubbed at his eyes and spat to clear his mouth between loudly excoriating the dung flinger; "Pah…you are a drinking bad fellow..Pah." I led the Parson down to the canal to cleanse his face and with my handkerchief I then removed any remaining material from the corner of his eye. A small audience had finally mustered in response to this commotion with one or two extending their interest to inspect the occupant of the dung heap. The clergyman had by now recovered his composure and he stood to address the villagers of West Dean with a censure that they should tolerate such drunkenness and human degeneracy. In response to this admonishment four geese waddled across the yard and with extended necks then hissed at the Parson whilst the onlookers soon dispersed and the snoring continued. The Parson thanked me for my assistance and stated that he must be on his way for he still had some distance to travel and yet make his return journey at a respectable hour. He then explained that he hoped to meet with a family of itinerants upon Whiteparish Common as he had made this same journey, on this date, with the exception of it falling upon a Sunday, for the last ten years and on only one occasion had he failed to locate his wandering congregation. I questioned whether these might be Gypsies or "Egyptians" as they have been termed, and the clergyman declared that this was indeed the case and he informed me that the Staveley family had accepted the Holy Bible and were receptive to prayer. Of a sudden I found myself making a request that I might accompany the Parson to which he readily granted his consent and we then hastily made our introductions and I can inform you my dear Uncle that I was now in the company of the Reverend Mr Dickson. There was a sense of urgency in his every action, from the retrieval of his horse to the clambering aboard the phaeton and I had no sooner stowed my pack and found my seat then we were clattering over a small bridge and I fancied that, in our wake, the curtain then closed upon the farce of the bankrupt canal.

You will recall that it was Colonel Boyle at the Woodyates Inn who had so had impressed upon me the notion of meeting with Gypsies when the opportunity arose and I now found myself in the company of one who was bent on their salvation. I was soon to learn that each and every one of us are sinners and are due to perish and face an eternity in H**l if gracious salvation is not immediately sought. I reasoned that the Parson would soon question my own spiritual dearth and so at the crest of a long chalk ridge I remarked upon the fine views available to the south before us and also, at our rear, a great forest extended for as far as my eye could tell. The Parson's eyes were still smarting from his encounter at the dung heap but his gaze was fixed firmly upon the road ahead and he confessed to little interest of distant views on either horizon. "Mr Chalk I do not travel to seek the picturesque in crags, vales and cataracts and yet I am aware there are many who hold an identical position to my own in our church and who care but little for their own flock and would eagerly seek distraction in such matters." As the clergyman urged on his hot and labouring horse it was clear that the Reverend Dickson ventured forth with only one purpose in mind and that was the saving of souls from eternal d**nation.

We forged ahead at reckless speeds along narrow lanes banked high with flourishing hedges, spared only from disaster at each twist in the road I believe by the divine purpose of our mission. We crossed the Romsey turnpike on the outskirts of a village called Whiteparish and then followed a poor road across the Common. This was indeed a curious place for it was neither a wood nor an open field and where single trees flourished with their many pole branches emerging in a cluster at a tall man's height from the ground. The trunks are made smooth by the interests and rubbing of animals and I saw geese, cows and horses scouring about this hard hoof pocked soil for a morsel to feed upon. Amongst these pole trees with their spring browning of flower and unfurling leaf are the dark rich green crowns of the spiky leafed holly, a tree that I can readily identify. A whiff of woodsmoke soon betrayed the presence of a cluster of simple canvas tents beside the road where perhaps three or more generations of one family of Gypsies had made their settlement. Our clattering arrival caused little surprise to the occupants of this sprawling encampment save for the barking of a number of lean dogs and indeed there were also cats, chickens with their chicks in tow and horses roaming about the place. All around lay evidence of the simple trades of the Gypsy with scattered chips of wood from the manufacture of carved spoons and pegs and also a hearth constructed of raised earth for metalwork with beside it a pair of hand bellows and a small stone anvil. A central fire smouldered with a timber tripod erected above it from which was suspended a large black pot. Amongst this haphazard industry children scampered about like kittens whilst mothers carried their very young tight to their hip in a band of cloth. From their various positions and activities the Staveley tribe slowly gathered together in silent anticipation, standing or squatting and a dog's growl was stifled by a single gruff command. The Parson swooped down from the phaeton and wasted no time upon introductions or explaining my presence to the reticent family and instead demanded the bible that he had bestowed upon them at an earlier visit. I remained beside the carriage as the bible was retrieved and presented to the visitor who with book in hand then visibly trembled as if the tome was a source of violent electricity. Whilst this conspicuous veneration was taking place one small boy found instead the plight of a thirsty horse an irresistible distraction and slipped away to return with a splash of water and presented this to the harnessed animal. Whilst the horse gratefully sucked at the pail the boy then laid a flat palm upon its stooped neck before looking up to study the stranger in the camp. I smiled at the boy but this had not the desired effect for he started and with a look of great consternation he then hastily returned to the family and hid amongst the legs of the elders. He then began whispering to others and pointing in my direction whilst also patting at his head. At first I could not comprehend this concern until another member of the tribe touched at his own hat and I then believed that the snake hatband must be the cause of this alarm and so I removed the snakecatcher's hat to prevent further disturbance. I wondered whether the desiccated snake had presented some form of bad omen for I knew not the lore or superstitions of the Gypsies and yet I believe that they had been truly unsettled by this occurrence. With the snakecatcher's hat placed upon the seat of the phaeton, the attention of the tribe was restored to the actions of the Parson who was now displaying the full force of his convictions before the apprehensive congregation. I had now the opportunity of studying the appearance of this burgeoning family and Colonel Boyle had warned of a grimy countenance upon the weathered faces of these out-of-doors dwellers and the darkness of their skin could not be truly determined as the soot and dust had created its own patina. The children stood shoeless and even a young woman displayed bare arms and feet and indeed the younger men and women were strong and handsome. There was no Englishness about these striking faces and common to all was the blackness of the hair and their eyes were as dark and mysterious as freshly broken flint. An elderly woman, who by virtue of her age must be the grandmother of the tribe, could not have displayed more wrinkles as she squinted into the sun at the clergyman whilst sucking upon the stump of her pipe. The continued silence of the family as they stood before the Parson was a measure of their guarded nature, and I could not begin to perceive what thoughts they held about the clergyman's drama or the references to the Old Testament for their faces betrayed no opinion. Despite this voluble expounding there was a great calmness about this church in the open air with birdsong abounding and these loud words, uncontained by any cavernous stone building, soon drifted away into the half wood. I wondered that it might indeed be I, the visitor, who was being shown a way, or a path through life for these travelling people had lived long enough on the periphery of our civilisation to follow the example of a sedentary life if they should wish it. I wondered how these wandering tribes would survive in a world empty of villages, towns, cities and of all constraints and boundaries. I believe that they might drift with the changing seasons, to gather and hunt and this ease of movement eschews the accumulation and encumbrance of belongings and also the requirement of the owning by deed the land under your feet. On our jolting journey to this place the Parson had spoken of "The unhappy plight of these itinerants and indeed if they might cease their eternal wandering and embrace the word of God then they may yet be free of their heathen customs and vices." As I studied closely the Staveley family I saw the grime upon their clothes and faces but I believe that there is a surety about their posture and also the knotted strength of a large family that will ensure their survival. I sense also that our presence creates a tension that will not abate until our departure.

The Clergyman then looked across at me as if unaware that I had not yet joined the congregation and he gestured with some impatience for me to leave my position and stand alongside the family. He then began the Lord's Prayer to which I was the only one who gave vocal support until the end when a low "Amen" was prised from the onlookers with a deal of encouragement. At the conclusion of the service the Parson stood and swayed in the bright sunshine with his head bowed whilst the itinerants shuffled and murmured amongst themselves. The pipe smoking grandmother then approached me and held flat her calloused palms and I did not comprehend her purpose until another woman gripped my wrists and I was made to show my own hands. I had thus far heard little of the language of these people but as they now gathered close around me I could hear the strange and rapid exchange of the most mysterious words. I knew not the purpose of this close inspection of my hand, called by the Staveley tribe a "dukering", but evidently the old woman took offence by what my palms revealed as her eyes widened and she uttered strange sounds that caused gasps and whispers amongst our audience. At this moment the Parson intervened and he forced his way through the tribe that had now encircled me "MR CHALK, MR CHALK..CEASE THIS AT ONCE". I was then pulled from the ring of Gypsies by the clergyman and severely reprimanded for participating in a heathen act when I should be still in quiet contemplation. "Mr Chalk you have done me a disservice and I now regret your presence here today." I sincerely apologised to the Reverend Dickson and by explanation I informed him that I had no notion of what had occurred and knew not that it was a bad thing. The clergyman's storm was quick to subside and he then explained that it was an old Gypsy tradition to read a stranger's fortune by the inspection of the lines and creases upon their palms and for this dubious service a coin is demanded in return. It was indeed this type of superstitious nonsense, explained the Parson, that good Christian teaching should soon dispel. He then declared that we must now depart for he had a good many miles to travel back to his own parish. As the Parson returned the bible to the elder of the family I inspected again my own palm to see if I could establish what had caused such alarm to the old pipe smoking woman to whom I was now in financial debt.

My dear Uncle my candle has just exploded which will explain the wax across the page and if I had not more to write then I would now gladly take to my bed but instead I have fumbled with flint, steel and tinder to enable me to resume my account for there is a grave conclusion to my meeting with the family of itinerants.

Before our departure from the encampment the Parson took a small package from the carriage and gave it to the grandmother for which she thanked him profusely. As the clergyman took his seat beside me he explained that each year he brought a gift of tea for the family and at the first visit he had made the mistake of participating in the drinking of it. He described how they would boil it all up and then pass this heavy stew of tea around in large tin bowls and he then made a face and shuddered at the memory of this experience. "Mr Chalk, it is another aspect of civilised life for which they require guidance."

With the sun at our backs we then lurched our way across the Common for there was to be no respite in the haste that the Parson required of his horse. I was soon shaken from my thoughts by the appearance of four horsemen approaching who arrested their charges and demanded that we also halted. These were militiamen and their Captain enquired as to the whereabouts of a tribe of Gypsies upon the Common to which the Parson explained that we had just now departed from their encampment for they were a family aspiring to be good Christians. The Captain laughed at this notion and declared that in his opinion they were all thieving blackguards and as the mounted militia then galloped on he called back "We shall soon see if they are good English Christians." The clergyman sat for a moment in silence and then rubbed at his chin before speaking. "In my experience, Mr Chalk, four horsemen shall never be the bearers of glad tidiings. We must return at once." As fast as we were able the Reverend Dickson reversed our course and began our race back along the rough and undulating track, in rapid pursuit of the militia. I too now feared what might become of the family and as we neared the encampment we could hear a great commotion with many raised voices. The tribe were mustered as before when in anticipation of the Parson's open air service and yet it was the barrel of a pistol that had now caused this herding together and not the promise of a packet of tea. Another dismounted Militiaman was slashing at the canvas tents with his sword and complaining loudly "G*d, they stink Sir, it would be a blessing to burn this filth. There's no Frenchie in 'ere". The Captain remained mounted as he observed the destruction of the Gypsy's few belongings and as a barking dog was kicked and a tethered ass released and thumped on the rump with the flat of a sword, this was too much for one young Gypsy and he flew at the uniformed assailant. The pair wrestled in the dust until another soldier brought the butt of his rifle down upon

the head of the itinerant to which he fell motionless upon
the ground. "ENOUGH, ENOUGH" roared the clergyman
as he rose up in the phaeton with the reins trembling in his
hands. "EXPLAIN THIS BARBARITY SIR." The Captain
of the militia drew level with the wide eyed Parson. "Calm
your fury Sir, for we are at War least you forget it and these..
good Christians of yours are known to harbour Frenchmen on
the run. A prisoner slipped our convoy at camp this morning
after burying himself in a fox's hole and I intend to hunt down
this French fox, take what may. Line up the men Sergeant,
surely you can tell apart a Frenchman from a Gypsy?"

As the women, children and older men huddled together,
the younger male Gypsies were made to speak out their names
to the Sergeant. The one who suffered the blow upon the head
was forced to stand also and swayed unsteadily, unable to
comprehend this new ordeal. Before further damage was
inflicted upon this unfortunate man the Parson leapt down
from his position and stood before the impatient sergeant. "If
you are to deal out more blows then you must strike me down
first and you shall then have God to answer to. Captain I have
known this family for ten years and observed these boys grow
to be men and I will swear before you upon the Holy Bible
that there is no Frenchman here, so help me."

I looked down upon the fear shown in the faces of the
children and hoped that the Parson's interjection would end
this ordeal. One small girl fumbled with an object and let it
fall to the ground at her feet before quickly stooping to retrieve

it and then concealed this piece within her garments. I knew at once that I had seen this self same object only hour's before as it had been offered to me by a desperate man in exchange for money as I had passed the convoy of French prisoners of war. It was a white carving of a figure, perhaps of bone and its presence here could mean only one thing. I was not alone in witnessing the falling of this object for the grandfather of the tribe now had his dark flinty eyes fixed upon my face and our gaze became locked and I was unable to look away until this eternity was broken by the call of the Captain to remount. "We have wasted enough time here" He called back "..and you, Parson, should keep better company in future."

As the thundering hooves departed I could not look up for I felt those same cold dark eyes still burning into my very soul and yet I was wholly aware of the treachery to my Nation that I had caused by not speaking out. I knew not what to do. The Frenchman had gone yet he had passed this way today leaving behind him the bone figure, perhaps his sole possession in a trade for food or clothing. What benefit to make captives of all these people for their brief harbouring of a desperate and helpless man? The Gypsy's nationality is obscure and it is as if they are foreigners in their own country and I had not the cold courage or conviction to bring further misery and mistreatment to these people. Should this lone Frenchman return to France and English lives become lost as a consequence then that blood would be forever on my hands.

I spoke of none of this to the clergyman who I believe

demonstrated the unstinting proof of his own conviction and acted with great bravery to spare further bloodshed. I hold nothing but admiration for his deed today and I believe that he contains within his body not one ounce of doubt regarding his purpose upon this earth.

I only wished to be released from the unblinking stare of the old Gypsy for he knew that I held their future in my hands and perhaps this was indeed the vision witnessed by the Gypsy grandmother after the sermon as she read with horror the lines upon my palms. The Parson wished to stay and assist with the reparations to the camp and yet the Staveley family urged him to depart, not with anger but so that they could repair themselves for I believe I have witnessed that strength today, of a family long used to facing adversity together.

At the turnpike I requested that I might be let down to find my own way. I then sincerely apologised to the Parson for he had good cause to admonish me and that I should never have requested to accompany him when my motive was but idle curiosity. This stern faced clergyman then surprised me greatly for he smiled as he took my hand. "Mr Chalk, if you have learnt something today then that is sufficient. We are all sinners after all but it is only those that forever seek salvation that may yet be saved. Go with God in your heart and you shall never be found wanting."

As the Parson turned a corner and disappeared from view I strode out upon the turnpike with much to dwell upon and walked in my lengthening shadow until I met with an inn that I believe lies in the neighbouring county of Hampshire. I know not what tomorrow holds for tonight I am but a hollow shell and weak of spirit.

Goodnight my dear Uncle, I pray that you will not judge me too harshly for I have openly confessed to you of my treachery. I hope and trust that you will understand when I tell you that I do not consider myself a traitor to the circumstances as they presented themselves and indeed how would you have acted in my stead?

I wonder that I shall ever understand my own purpose upon this earth save for the abiding love that I hold for another.

Your confused nephew
HENRY CHALK

My dear Uncle,

I have just climbed from my bed and I can report that pedestrianism and sleeping exhaust in equal measure. I awoke in a tangle of hot and twisted sheets believing that I had already made some reparations for my treacherous silence before the militia at the Gypsy encampment by now enlisting for the army. In my tormented dream I had been packed tight amongst a thousand men aboard a ship and then endured a stormy voyage before rowing ashore to face a wild eyed foe. Our force was ill equipped against thunderous guns and long slashing swords for we each had only a knife and a fork to make our defence. I recall my protestations to a most senior Commander that the inferior quality of Sheffield goods would not do and we must in its stead utilise the best steel cutlery from the workshops of Mr Henry Shorto in Salisbury. I was swiftly cast in irons for my insubordination for I had no notion that the General was a proud native of Sheffield and a stout defender of its modern industry.

There is much early activity at this Inn of which I still do not know the name and I would rest further but a weary gentleman traveller has just entered the room and upon eyeing my vacant bed has swiftly claimed it for himself. The blankets and hot damp sheets are hauled in vain across his head and this bed thief now makes a weak groan against the cruel probing of the morning sun.

The day has begun without a purpose and I can think of no destination that hurries me to my breakfast and yet I have been spared further torment for I am no longer that clammy and writhing lump aboard the creaky bed.

I have thrown open the window to attract a fresh draught of air into this small room for the malign gusts within have greatly increased with the arrival of my uninvited guest.

The ink is flowing freely from the pen at this early hour and once the nib is charged above the page and thoughts are already formed in that glob of black liquid then there is but little labour required in the task of writing. I believe that I must avail myself of this opportunity for I have some explaining to do if I may impose further upon your time.

I have promoted to you my dear Uncle that the purpose of my return to this mysterious county of Wiltshire has been the search for flint of a fine quality that would satisfy the needs of our ancient ancestors. I have not been disingenuous for that is indeed the case and in addition I have the great pleasure of a first meeting with Robert Foster at the Winterslow Hut. I have indicated that whilst brother and sister are estranged then no longer can I communicate directly with Sarah Foster and this hiatus has also presented an opportunity to continue with my pedestrianism and the spilling of yet more ink upon the page. Sir, I have given you two good reasons but I fear that I have been reticent upon the manner of my leaving the home of Mr Richard Fenton in the county of Pembrokeshire. There is indeed a third reason for my being abroad in Wiltshire and I feel bound to present to you the facts that hastened my departure from that place near two weeks ago. Mr John Fenton, as you will recall, is a young master in the art of raillery and I have before suffered for the sake of his own idle amusement. I truly believe that he expects reciprocation in equal measure and yet I am not built that way and would gain little pleasure in such combat. Defeat for John Fenton exists in my indifference to these pitfalls and mantraps that he lays out before me for they are now to be expected at any moment of timely distraction. I am forever on my guard in his company and yet we may walk and talk and become an amicable pair to the casual observer for there is much that is of mutual interest. There was a mustering of friends at Glynamel and Mr Richard Fenton was not present for he had returned again to London. Mrs Eliza Fenton arranged an admirable table in the gardens as the weather had just become fair and there was much amusement with singing and games. I was chosen to become blind man's buff and then spun around relentlessly until dizziness near overcame me and the tight scarf across my eyes let in not even the smallest portion of light. I did not rove about with my hands before me but stood inanimate for a good while longer than any previous participant on that afternoon. I at first tried to tell my direction from the faint wind upon my cheek until the slamming of the front door betrayed the position of the house and my orientation was then established. The distant chiming of bells informed me that it was three o'clock and I began to believe that our eyes make very short work of the world around us. Before the blindfold had been attached I had only thoughts of preparing the garden and with the arrival of guests, as one is wont to do, I began the study of unfamiliar faces. In the blackness I now distinguished between voices that were known to me and also the tones of strangers who possessed the lilting sing-song richness of the Cambrian accent. Amongst this chattering and a clattering of cups upon saucers there existed also a furious industry of insects and birds in the garden and this rich orchestra of sounds soared about my head. The children then goaded me into moving slowly forward and yet I was not seeking to catch the nearest and boldest of the players for I was thinking all the while of Sarah and her perpetual blindfold. It was through all these sensations that I then heard the voice of John Fenton, not in a loud and mischievous manner but a portion of whispered conversation that was assuredly not meant for my ears. "..He has but a bankrupt and untrustworthy Uncle for a family and the poor lamb cherishes the love of a blind girl. We must therefore be charitable towards our young pedestrian." I know not to whom he was talking and it matters little for it was the earnest manner and attempt at discretion that made the effect of his words one thousand times worse than any taunt or intended cruelty.

The birds ceased their singing and the crockery and

children's laughter became silent also for the thundering inside my head replaced all these things. John Fenton did not witness the removal of the blindfold for he had become distracted by the arrival of a mother and daughter into the garden and it was the latter that was receiving his full attention. The children were quickly drawn towards chasing a playful puppy into the shrubbery and I stood alone upon the lawn shielding my blinking and watery eyes against the bright afternoon. I soon retired to the house and sat upon my bed without knowing what to do with myself and yet I could not remove John Fenton's whispered words from my thoughts. I cannot believe that discussions have taken place between Mr Richard Fenton and his son John regarding my most private affairs. I have entrusted the details of my meeting with Sarah Foster to no one other than her brother Robert and can only gauge that John Fenton has spied upon my correspondence and secretly availed himself of the nature of her affliction. Such behaviour is surely despicable but not I fear beyond the capabilities of this young man for he has before taken my unsealed letters and read them in my presence when I could not prevent it. I know not also what he means by branding you Sir as untrustworthy! What an affront on your good character by one who has proved himself not to be trustworthy himself. I wished now that I were bold and brave and had challenged John Fenton in his garden to demand an explanation. I wonder that I shall ever boil over in anger and let my actions speak out for themselves as to be timid all ones life will gain respect from no quarter. Indeed if Mr Richard Fenton had been present then I may still be at Glynamel for he would surely get to the bottom of these most serious of issues and then admonish strongly his son's indiscretion. Instead I packed my bag, leaving behind all that I could not comfortably carry on my back and also retrieved my thumbstick from the hallway before departing. I was but a few paces from the house when I realised that I could not leave without speaking first with Mrs Eliza Fenton for I had become a very welcome guest in her household these last few months and she was indeed deserving of some explanation. The afternoon visitors had long departed and I found the mistress of the house busy at her writing desk and as I did not wish to disturb Mrs Fenton I quietly made my retreat but she paused to ask who was there. I entered the room fully and yet I found that I could not state my true purpose and instead I commended Mrs Fenton upon the success of the day to which she concurred that the weather had again been favourable to the event and they were indeed most fortunate. There was then a moment of silence before I thanked Mrs Eliza Fenton sincerely although I do not believe that she knew for what purpose my gesture was intended and I hastily departed to enable her to continue unhindered in her writing. I fully intend to write to both Mr and Mrs Fenton to give some account of my actions and whereabouts for I believe that there must be some concern as to the abruptness of my departure and its cause.

From Fishguard I took the evening coach to Milford for

I had already constructed a feeble plan that I soon failed to execute. I recalled that Mr Richard Fenton had once made a sea voyage across to Minehead upon the Somersetshire coast departing from Milford aboard a small packet ship. Once at the home of Miss Sarah Foster I would announce myself boldly at the front door and all would be very well indeed. I have already advised you Sir that it was a feeble plan, burgeoning with desperation and short on discretion and therefore doomed to failure. On arriving at Milford I found lodging at the Lord Nelson Hotel which is a large and newly built establishment. Indeed it is altogether a new town constructed to the design of the Hon Mr Charles Greville and there is a great deal more to observe in Milford than at lowly Fishguard for the harbour is alive with small vessels. In the dockyards below the town great naval ships are under construction with these infant vessels resting in their giant cradles, the progeny of our war with France and they attract the interest of all who visit Milford. I was most surprised to learn that it is a Frenchman, Monsieur Barralier, who is assisting with the building of these English warships for he is a nobleman that fled "Le Terror" and is now an architect in thwarting the grand schemes of the little Corsican. My dear Uncle, I did not bring you to Milford for any other purpose but to explain my progress from the Fenton household. It was indeed my intention to depart for Somersetshire as soon as possible for in my troubled mind I was able to consider no other course of action and it was as well that upon my arrival at Milford I hastily put pen to paper and wrote to Robert Foster in London explaining all that had passed. That I should still be in Milford to receive his reply I have the simple oyster to thank. I can report that good fortune and extreme discomfort were contained within the shell of this little creature for one dose kept me in and out of my bed for three days and nights. Upon the fourth day I was able to shuffle meekly to the window and observe through my telescope the Waterford Packet arrive and then slowly depart for all wind had ceased and the sails upon the bay were as limp as my own constitution. The arrival of a letter from Mr Robert Foster in London then provided the best tonic of all for it contained sweet hope and plans and there is nothing more essential to raise the spirit than hope and plans. It was Robert Foster's suggestion that I should again prosecute a pedestrian excursion to my favoured County of Wiltshire. Some five years ago the Foster family found sanctuary from a snow blizzard at the Wintersow Hut whilst on a journey from London and as this establishment was known to Robert Foster he believed that we should make our first acquaintance there for he was soon to return again from the Capital City. I could not reply swiftly enough to commend him on this suggestion and was able to pack my belongings and depart from unfinished Milford leaving behind a measurable degree of my own substance for my clothes were now made loose by the effects of that blessed oyster. I suffered uncomfortable and halting progress before gaining a crossing of the River Severn at the New Passage and thereon my journey became hot and cramped to Bristol,

Bath and Shaftesbury. Upon entering into Wiltshire I felt my old self again and had no longer the scent of rotten low tide in my nostrils and I shall consign oysters to a list of undesirables that already contains beer and port wine.

The bed thief here in this little room has woken from his sketchy slumber and after clawing back the sheets from around his head has now the impudence to scowl that the scratching and scraping of my pen is playing with his nerves. He seeks the chamber pot, a prospect that prompts my own swift vacation.

*

I have this afternoon arrived at the Winterslow Hut that is perched beside the busy London road and it is the desire to hear news of my beloved Sarah from her trusted brother that has guided me to this place. At the sound of each approaching stage I survey the yard below for a passenger that I know will not arrive for two more days and I curse again this absurd expectation. My journey is ill planned for Robert is not expected until Friday 13th and it is surely better to be busy with pedestrianism than laying idle in a coaching house. I shall at least receive some grateful shelter from the pounding sun and escape from the curious and alarming circumstances that have plagued this troublesome correspondent whilst he is abroad in the open country. I sincerely hope that to settle a while at the Winterslow Hut will keep the hounds of adventure from snapping at my heels for this appears a very ordinary place.

So what of my day? Curiosity demanded that I first retraced my steps of yesterday and I found myself again crossing Whiteparish Common and passing between the scant concealment of the trees until I could gain a vantage point. I lamented again the loss of my looking glass for it was an occasion well suited to this surreptitious behaviour. My anticipation was in vain for the encampment was no more and gone were the ripped open tents, the animals and also the great strangeness brought to this place by the itinerant Staveley family. I felt no mystery still lingering upon this spot for that exists with the tribe and will inhabit the next verge or glade where tents are raised and where animals feely graze. A warm hearth and a scattering of woodchips were all that remained behind and I did not care to investigate further over the detritus of these perpetual wanderers. I wondered whether they would ever return to Whiteparish Common and again produce the bible upon the arrival of the stern faced Reverend Dickson. In truth I believe that it was the prospect of encountering the yellow clad Frenchman that drew me back to this now vacated encampment as if he might be sitting pondering upon a stump and awaiting my arrival to escort him back to his place of detention. I can report that he was nowhere to be seen and I was therefore unable to make amends for my treachery. Indeed the prospect of a flash of yellow in the corner of my eye kept me in a state of great vigilance as I continued on my way until I then stumbled upon some fashioned flint in the grounds of Breach House whereupon my distraction was easily won and complete. The earth here is sandy with flint pebbles but it is also patchy with evidence of a heavy clay that is now dried and cracked. Hidden amongst trees and thick undergrowth a river has once gouged its deep course but today I found a mere rusty trickle between small shingle banks that enabled me to hop along the revealed bed in perfect concealment from the fields on either side. I clambered from this secret watery passage with caution for I knew not upon whose private land I was freely wandering. I then spied a planted field and amongst this exposed soil I scraped and probed with my thumbstick, turning over smooth pebbles and prising out promising lumps for inspection whilst trying to avoid crushing the sprouting crop under my boot. The flint here is stained a honey brown and yet these rounded pebbles retain a freshness despite this attractive opacity. That they have been stained, rolled and rounded by their longevity amongst water there can be little doubt, but I believed that this ready supply of flint in the river bed and upon its fringe must have been freely exploited by our early ancestors. I wished to prove this theory to myself and the longer I scoured the ground for evidence to support this fact the more determined I became in my search. I could hear a boy calling and hurling his rattle about to keep the birds from the nearby crop and yet I was not to be deterred from my quest. I at last retrieved a broken slither of flint and felt a tremble at this reassurance as my close inspection revealed its sharpness and slender regularity. There is also a feature of any piece of flint that has been purposefully struck from the parent block for it displays a small pimple on its underside at the exact point of this impact and it is a record left upon the stone itself of this moment of detachment. I pushed my thumbstick into the soil to mark the spot where I had found the flint slither and began a closer scouring of the ground. I thought back to Peter Winter beside the flint pit in Grovelly as he worked at his gunflints and the fast accumulating mass of waste flint detritus that lay about his feet. The great passage of time, the earthworm and the disruption of the plough will bury and disperse these working clusters and yet a proportion will remain if sought closely enough. I was indeed rewarded for my perseverance for I spied a pebble that displayed the equal and parallel scars of these purposeful fractures. It was once the shape of a large egg and indeed its dark outer rind is no thicker than that of an egg shell. The flint inside is now as cloudy and grey as a sky upon a stormy day but I wager that when this piece was last held and struck open the revealed flint was bright and uniform. I then collected a complete pebble from the soil and another larger broken piece to act as a blacksmiths anvil. A third pebble was required for a hammer and with three blows I had shattered the complete pebble and was able to confirm the fresh regularity of the flint within. My concentration upon the soil beneath my feet had drawn me across two fields and I found myself conducting my noisy experiment within full view of a very large red brick house with only an ornamental lake between my position and the grand façade of the building. The chinking of the flint had attracted the attention of the gardener who was busy shaping a large hedge and he called out to me across the water. More heads popped up from amongst this hedge and there was evidently a team of workers employed to the task. His exact words were not apparent but by his gesticulations I gathered that I should not be roaming about the master's field and so I quickly pocketed my prized flints and politely waved before continuing on my way. The white shirted man was soon intent upon my pursuit and once he began to round the lake and was lost from my view behind some greenery, I then changed my direction to return from whence I came. My devious turnabout was loudly reported to the white shirt by his team of lookouts aboard the hedge but in that time I was able to retreat to the secret passage of the sunken river bed and retrace my steps without fear of having to break out again into open ground. I thought this the end of the matter until I heard dogs barking with men calling loudly and my stomach turned with the realisation that there was now a genuine intent upon my capture. I hastened my pace splashing on through deeper pools, pressing farther up this narrow and twisting gorge all the while cursing how preciously these county gentlemen guarded their property. A large tree had fallen to lay slumped from bank to bank and I was required to duck down low to pass beneath it but forgetting my pack I then became ensnared amongst the stubs of its broken branches. In a wild panic I struggled the pack from my shoulder and heaved it beyond this obstacle to hear it splash heavily upon the other side. As I emerged from under this spiky and resinous tree my heart gave a great leap for my eyes set upon a pair of old and broken shoes, ragged breaches and then as I raised my head further an old patched shirt. To complete this picture of wretchedness a man with a bony face and sunken fearful eyes stood swaying and gasping before me. Of a sudden he became overcome with weakness and fell to his knees in a pool of rusty water and shook his head in desperation. I knew in an instant that I had encountered the emaciated form of the escaped Frenchman that had only yesterday offered me a carved bone figure in Alderbury. His hours of freedom had now come to an end for he had not the strength to walk another step. From my pack I quickly extracted a half loaf of dry bread that I had secreted from the breakfast table and also a handful of coins from my purse and I thrust these things with some urgency towards the man. He nodded slowly in acknowledgement and with a realisation that I was also by some manner a fugitive he whispered hoarsely "Allee, Allee" and indicated that I should depart with haste. He then rolled back against the bank and tore weakly at the crumbling bread and with the barking dogs splashing ever closer I clambered up the bank and darted away between the trees. I did not turn to witness the apprehension of the French prisoner of war but I could hear well enough the great crescendo of barking and the raised excited calls of the pursuers that heralded their victorious discovery. I lessened my pace and in a short while rested up against a tree to draw breath and to wipe the coating of sweat from my face. That the triumphant hunting party would return immediately to Breach House I held no doubt and none would question how their quarry might have altered from a pedestrian tourist to become a fugitive Frenchman. I now believe that the roaming militia would have informed widely of the presence of the escaped prisoner of war and therefore any stranger at large would have been viewed with great suspicion. By the clashing together of flint pebbles I have caused the capture of this man and as a consequence I have played my unwitting part in his apprehension. Any blight on my conscience could therefore be expunged forthwith and yet all was not so settled in my own mind. When confronted with the plight of such a pathetic and desperate soul is not the human and indeed the Christian instinct to provide help and succour? I believe that the Staveley family supplied clothes to the fugitive and perhaps such sustenance that they were able to give. I sincerely hope that the captors at Breach House gave food and drink to strengthen the nameless Frenchman for I consider that he would surely die without it.

At a safe distance from Breach House I left the rusty river behind me and in time crossed the Southampton turnpike. I then found myself walking the same narrow lanes along which I had rattled only yesterday with such urgent fervour beside the Reverend Dickson. I know not at what stage I took the decision to proceed to the Winterslow Hut or indeed whether

I made any such decision at all for in the heat my head had become a vacant shell. Upon John Cary's heavily folded map I have travelled not one little fingers length from the Inn upon the Romsey road and yet it has been a hard day's toil. I longed that a great cloud might appear to cast a roving shadow across the land and I could then chase that shade all the day to keep my skin from the burning sun. No such cloud arrived and my face is now dry and nut brown and I do not believe you would know me from a shepherd or indeed a gypsy if we had the good fortune to meet upon the road. There is everywhere a preoccupation with the weather for it is either "Unreasonably hot" or "Nation warm snaw" depending on whether the commentator might be fanning a flushed face at the breakfast table or leaning upon a farm gate. The beasts in the field are presumably similarly engaged across fences and hedges upon the subjects of irritating flies and a shortage of mud to roll about in.

My weary legs drew me to the sensible shade of the fringes of any wood that I had the good fortune to encounter and I paused to slumber a while in a thick and busy hedge amongst the rustlings and flutterings of the creatures there.

On approaching the Winterslow Hut I dusted myself down and prepared for an indifferent reception but on crossing the threshold I could detect raised voices and it proved to be a suitable distraction for the landlady was in the throws of an altercation with a disgruntled gentleman.

"Madam, you are most disobliging. It is after all a simple

matter."

"Loike I say, I aint n'thas that."

The troubled gentleman stood with his back towards me and shuffled uncomfortably before the intransigent and purse lipped landlady.

"I shall write to the Salisbury Postmaster in the strongest terms."

It appeared that no amount of sighing, shuffling and remonstration was about to persuade the landlady from concluding the delivery of this gentleman's correspondence and it was to stubbornly remain at the inn for his collection. At this juncture I surprised myself by stepping from the shadows to promote a bold suggestion.

"Madam. Sir. May I offer albeit a temporary solution, for the short duration of my stay here at the Winterslow Hut, I should be willing to deliver any correspondence to this gentleman personally. Indeed I should welcome the task for I have little to occupy me until the anticipated arrival of a dear friend from London on the thirteenth day of this month."

In the silence that followed I hastily pressed on with my ingratiation towards the landlady and removed the snakecatcher's hat. "Madam, Henry Chalk of Southwark at your service."

I then turned to the dark haired and furrow browed gentleman who consistently refused to meet my eye and he offered eventually the limpest of hands that could not satisfactorily be shaken. After scowling once more at the landlady and recovering his flaccid hand, this abrupt and unhappy gentleman then turned upon his heal and swiftly attempted his departure only to find the latch upon the front door equally uncooperative and he cursed that also. I then pursued the landlady to play upon the tentative understanding that my offer to conclude the delivery of the gentleman's mail had in some way now become a silent acceptance and as to my own right of accommodation.

"Madam, I did not catch the gentleman's name..if I am to..?"

The landlady spun about to face me with arms still tightly folded; "'Is name is Asslit. Newly weds 'pon the 'ill n I aint deliverin' no mail n' thas a fact. Landlord be round presently".

Muttering to herself, the landlady then shuffled away beyond the public domain and in time a slender and taciturn landlord appeared and found little fault in accommodating a dusty pedestrian tourist. Indeed by his weary demeanour I believe that he has witnessed all that there is to witness beside the busy London road.

*

So, my dear Uncle here I am at the Winterslow Hut and I have just heard some late arrivals enter the building and could not resist a casual inspection and there are none that would match a description of Robert Foster for they are all older travellers. Their eventual destination is Powderham Castle near the City of Exeter yet one of their party has swollen legs and they have been forced to spend the night here and not continue on to Salisbury. It is one of the few pleasures of such establishments, to observe others who are all thrown together in the haphazard business of travel. There are those who are sociable and enjoy this tumult and revel in the opportunity to make merry with their fellow men and then there are those that perceive the whole as a necessary evil that is to be endured and are curt in their dealings with staff and guests alike. The new arrivals were four in number yet the one with "legs swelled like capstans" had already taken to his bed and the three remaining gentlemen were left to enjoy a late supper.

"He would be better dealt with in Salisbury. Better lodging and better company and I should require a fire."

"A fire Sir! Look at you. I believe that I could boil a kettle on your pate if you would only oblige by first removing that cosy that passes for a wig. A fire indeed."

"Mr Curtis is a great friend of the fire and he thinks it purifies the air and that his fine constitution is living proof."

"Is it also true Mr Curtis that you wear six waistcoats in both summer and winter?"

"If you believe gentlemen that you can gain your entertainment by the mocking of my sensible habits then I suggest that you have neither enough wit nor brain between you to contrive even a rudimentary conversation."

"Ha. We shall see about that. I suggest then that poetry is superior to painting. What say you Mr Pilkington"

"Indeed Mr Snape? Then how so the poet Wordsworth has

not made more than one hundred and sixty pounds by all his labours when any mediocre portrait painter can appease the vanity of his subject for that much alone?"

"It is not simply a question of money Mr Pilkington, I wager that Wordsworth is driven to write and would do so if there were not a soul to read it."

"Hmm. I maintain Mr Snape that a painting will sit quietly upon the wall and behave itself. Poets are an unsettling breed and poetry forces one to smile in a sickly way as you are obliged to pretend that you understand it."

"I grant Mr Pilkington that poetry can never be wholly understood by anyone but can it not express love better than any daubing? Our mind will deal in words and they shall haunt and surface again when by contrast we need to be forever placed before even the very best of paintings to be reminded of their worth."

" Gentlemen, gentlemen, as you have concocted your laborious dialogue for my benefit then I shall determine that Mr Reynolds is a great painter and Mr Coleridge a wind bag and now I shall seek a fire even if I have to break the furniture into little pieces and place it in the grate myself. Goodnight Sirs, I wish I could express my pleasure by your company but it is like the revolting hard water of this cursed place, to be endured."

Sir, I realise that I have parted company with my thumbstick and yet I do not believe that I shall return to the grounds of Breach House to continue with my investigations nor to retrieve my stick from the soil for I may easily cut another. Let it be a simple monument to the capture of the French fugitive for without my clashing together of flint pieces at that very spot then he may still be at large. I shall not forget the very sobering events of these last two days for it has given me much to ponder upon. I now have these sandy examples of fashioned flint set before me and I intend to give exercise to the pencil and make a careful study of them. I consider that ancient man gathered flint where need arose and opportunity occurred and would perhaps return over and again to the rusty river and other such fruitful places. My "tour in search of flint" continues but I have been thrown a gobbet of encouragement by my simple finds amongst the soils of Breach House.

I shall now exchange the pen for the pencil and I wish you goodnight.

Your faithful nephew
Henry Chalk

Thursday 12th May 1808

MY DEAR UNCLE,

This morning I have received a letter of apology from Robert Foster to inform me that he has suffered a delay in his plans. He shall not now appear until Sunday 15th of May and all is frustration. This news has further exposed the folly of my early arrival at the Winterslow Hut. I have little to occupy me save for the task of transporting fresh correspondence to the home of the ungrateful and irascible gentleman who lives upon the hill in Middle Winterslow. It is a Wiltshire custom of speech to remove the "H" at any opportunity to satisfy the lust for an "Aaah" or an "Eee" so despite the Landlady's taut lipped insistence that the Gentleman's name is Asslit, I see from the letters before me that it is indeed Mr William Hazlitt. With this understanding I now believe that my thumbstick is cut from the hazel bush and is not spelt "azel" as I first thought.

On my return I must write to Mr and Mrs Fenton for a letter of explanation, however difficult that may be to compose, is long overdue.

I rapped upon the door of the small cottage in Middle Winterslow and was swiftly confronted by a portion of Mr William Hazlitt who then fidgeted impatiently with the door ajar as if he had been rudely disturbed. Presented with this awkwardness and his strangely averted gaze I did not at first declare my purpose and instead bid the gentleman a fine morning.

At this juncture a lady's voice could be heard enquiring from within.

"Who is it William?"

Mr Hazlitt paused to study my boots before answering.

"I do not know. He proposes that it is a fine morning when it is patently not so for the air is too heavy."

"What does he want?"

I then thrust the two carried letters towards the aperture between frame and door and reminded Mr Hazlitt that I had only yesterday afternoon promised to deliver his correspondence for the short duration of my stay at the Inn.

The heavy brow puckered in confusion.

"He brings my letters from the Hut."

"Then give him a coin. Do you have a coin?"

At this point Mr Hazlitt was pushed to one side and replaced at the now fully opened door by Mrs Hazlitt who with long fingers then delved into a soft pouch in search of a coin. I removed the snakecatcher's hat and hastily introduced myself, explaining my offer of yesterday which halted her probing for the elusive gratuity.

"Then that is most kind. William, Mr Chalk is himself a guest at the Hut. William?"

Mr Hazlitt had since lost interest in the events at the front door and could be heard thumping and bumping elsewhere in the small house. His wife sighed in resignation as if this misunderstanding could have been easily averted. "You must wonder at Mr Hazlitt's strangeness. I am drinking tea, would you care for some tea Mr Chalk? Please do at least come in and drink some tea. William? We have a young guest."

I followed Mrs Hazlitt into the parlour where crates brimming with books were strewn about and a pleasant smell of turpentine hung in the air. Upon the bare floor a number of small canvasses stretched upon frames were turned to face the wall and I took these to be paintings although I could not gauge their subject nor their stage of completeness. A cup was found and books were then removed from a chair and also a space cleared at the table to enable me to join Mrs Hazlitt in drinking tea.

My hostess must have then caught my eye looking about the place for she laughed as tea was poured and in truth I had not before witnessed such domestic turmoil and neither could I judge the standing of Mr and Mrs Hazlitt in their small cottage. "We have been married barely a week Mr Chalk and there is much to do so please forgive our disarray but it is largely of my husband's making for there was some order to this place before his arrival."

I then stood and offered my warm congratulations to the news of their recent marriage much to the amusement of Mr Hazlitt who had just reappeared. "It is a husband's duty to disrupt. It is what we do best".

"Do you think him rude Henry? Mr Hazlitt is not at all a model husband."

In referring to me as Henry and to her husband as Mr Hazlitt, Mrs Hazlitt had created for me a place of curious intimacy in their relationship, as if I were now in some manner a confidant. I returned to my seat and found some simple reassurance in cradling a warm cup.

Mrs Hazlitt explained that her husband was an author and also a painter and sometimes he could not decide which.

"Today I do not know which course he will take but he will soon declare that he must go out and traverse the countryside with only his thoughts for company and leave me to his unholy mess."

Indeed as if to confirm this unhusbandly behaviour Mr Hazlitt passed by the table with boots in hand and a black notebook under his arm.

As there had been no enquiry forthcoming as to my own occupation or purpose here in Winterslow I then informed Mrs Hazlitt that I was a pedestrian tourist and that there was no finer County than Wiltshire in which to make such excursions.

"Why then Sir..." enquired Mr Hazlitt as he completed the lacing up of his boots "..are you clucking and drinking tea in our parlour when the fine County awaits?"

This curious Gentleman then placed his hat and rattled open the cottage door before pausing for a brief moment to suggest that he wished that Mrs Hazlitt would let her hair grow long. The door was then firmly slammed behind him and his quickly departing paces could be heard in the silence that settled upon the parlour.

I slowly drained my cup as Mrs Hazlitt then sighed and shook her head wearily, "Always thinking and walking, walking and thinking. I believe that he is also married to the barren wastes and woods of Winterslow."

I did not wholly believe that Mr Hazlitt's remark, made whilst lacing his boots, had been a formal invitation for me to accompany him and yet it may have been construed as such from any other reasonable mortal. It was however a situation of grave impropriety to be left alone in the company of Mrs Hazlitt and therefore any reason for a swift departure was to be sorely welcomed. Salvation came in the unlikely form of the snakecatcher's hat that I placed upon the cluttered table and Mrs Hazlitt's gaze settled upon this curious object and her eyes then grew wide in consternation.

"Your hat..?"

I apologised for my ill mannered behaviour and quickly retrieved the battered and shapeless hat from the table.

"You..You have a snake upon your hat.. and ..there.. beneath it lay Mr Hazlitt's pencils. He will be in a rage once he requires his pencils."

"Madam, I must make amends and transport Mr Hazlitt's pencils immediately for I am at fault. Please excuse me."

With this Heaven sent opportunity I pushed back my chair and snatched up the pencils in their cloth wrap whilst Mrs Hazlitt pursued me to the door calling out; "Follow him Mr Chalk, follow and see where he goes. He has a fine pair of legs and you will do well to keep pace."

I had no genuine obligation to continue for I could sensibly return the pencils tomorrow and yet the fast disappearing form of Mr William Hazlitt soon caused me to skip along and lengthen my usual ponderous stride in order to keep sight of him. I had not my pack to slow me down nor duties that would suffer by further procrastination and indeed I had now become invigorated by tea and curiosity.

From a tree crowded church atop a hill to a church resting comfortably on the valley floor, we marched a good mile with Mr Hazlitt looking neither left nor right and most certainly not behind him. In the neighbouring village to Winterslow, ancient observers at the doors of simple mud and chalk houses slowly turned their heads as not one but two strange fellows passed them by with some unaccountable distance set between them. We crossed a road and began our ascent once more upon a worn trail that led to I knew not where. In the deep chequered shade of trees and bushes the dark striding figure ahead tugged me from the distraction of rounded flint pebbles in the soil and the study of curious flora upon the verges. The path dipped again as we passed a labourers cottage, deathly quiet in its sequestered vale where a rabbit and a pedestrian startled one another in near collision. In time my legs told of gradients achieved and signalled the reaching of a plateau within the wood for muscles eased and breathing was again regular. The vegetation soon became green and lush with oaks trees abounding and I gauged that the settled clay upon this chalk ridge was now of a good depth with moisture retained in the heavy bright ochre soil. It occurs to me, my dear Uncle, that where a mass of thick flinty clay has been curiously retained upon these highest South Wiltshire chalk ridges then it may have provided ancient man with a suitable source from which to form his early stone tools. When flint is kept moist by spending an eternity on a river bed or upon the seas shore or indeed when it is protected amongst this thick ochreous clay then its purposefulness may be retained. By this same token flint must therefore dry out if conditions are not favourable and this is a circumstance that I must commit to Mr Henry Shorto of Salisbury for he is soon to embark upon a full study of this most mysterious substance. I wished to deviate from the path ahead and search about for fresh flint amongst the root balls of fallen trees and yet I had become enslaved in this preposterous and unrelenting pursuit.

A bank rose up upon the northern fringe of this woodland plateau and in the brightness beyond the thinning trees lay the promise of distant views.

The figure ahead then deviated from his course to enter an open and curiously undulating place where buildings with solid walls had once stood but there now remained only the crumbling stumps of their foundation concealed amongst bushes and strangled by ivy. Upon every rabbit throw lay broken red brick and tile fragments and you may well imagine my great curiosity at this discovery. Standing defiantly amidst this decay a single segment of wall, perhaps an end wall, constructed of densely packed flint and greensand stone had survived the years. As I approached to inspect this impressive remnant all was quiet save for the soft jangling of sheep bells in the distance and I had become quite distracted from my pursuit of Mr Hazlitt and indeed knew not what had become of him. Whilst rounding this monolith I did not show due attention to my footing and then stumbled over part of the fallen debris of the wall and ended sprawled upon my knees before the seated Mr Hazlitt who then justly sprang up in exclamation;

"WHAT ..WHAT.. WHO.. What in goodness name are you about?."

I had not the breath to utter a word for a moment and Mr Hazlitt continued his protest whilst pacing back and forth; "Are you.. are you mad?... You deliver my letters and then.. and then..creep about for how many miles to make me jump from my skin. Explain yourself Sir."

I returned to my feet and then dusted the small embedded stones from my grazed palms before stating meekly; "I have your pencils Sir."

"What do you mean you have my pencils? I have my pencils. What tomfoolery is this?"

"I placed my hat upon your table.."

"What has your hat to do with it?"

"..and concealed your pencils beneath it. I have your pencils."

We then both went to our pockets where I soon retrieved the cloth wrap of pencils and held them out before me whilst Mr Hazlitt patted and pulled out pocket linings in his prolonged and fruitless search.

"You have my pencils." Conceded Mr Hazlitt.

With this resolution we then sat down upon the grass and for an age not another word was spoken.

This was not an awkward silence or one of embarrassment but a silence acceptable to both. I have indeed spent long enough at walking and pondering to recognise a moment when the body is content to be idle after exertion and the mind shall drift happily enough on its own. The spirit of a place may at such times waft into the mind's ether and perhaps of such fine gossamer poetry is spun. A poet may gather and fashion this delicate fabric but it will not survive my clumsy grasp and by the first thrust of a pen becomes torn and lays in ruin upon the page. You will recall, my dear Uncle, the letter mislaid by the young lady of Ferne House that contained poetry of such precious beauty and indeed I cannot now return to my lumpish prose when I again write to my beloved Sarah after the example set by one "Percy Bysshe". I have conducted a hapless search for any such latent gift but must concede that poets are born and cannot simply learn their craft as might a cobbler, cutler or brewer's clerk. Mr William Hazlitt has I believe the measure of me and was the first to break our pact of silence.

"As you are a tourist Mr Chalk then you will require information and explanation for is that not what all tourists seek? I take it that you are not acquainted with this place?

Nor I, but I have passed it by on my walk to Salisbury when I first visited Winterslow."

Mr Hazlitt went on to explain that it was a place where the Norman Kings enjoyed their regal privilege; to hunt and feast and to plot against those who defied them.

"Thomas Becket died in Canterbury Cathedral but he was surely murdered the instant that King Henry the Second uttered his fatal instruction…"

Mr Hazlitt leapt up and then manoeuvred himself centrally before the remaining wall of the ruined Palace. "..Perhaps.. here, Mr Chalk, for where else would a King be placed but at the end of the Great Hall, seated upon his Royal dias? You have Mr John Britton's Beauties of Wiltshire to thank for these bare bones and I have added the dramatic flesh…for the benefit of the tourist and pencil bearer."

Mr Hazlitt then removed himself from the remains of the Great Hall and strolled about for views and angles from which to make future paintings and concluded that it was not sufficiently Picturesque and a more Gothic ruin would suit better with perhaps a blasted tree.

Having dismissed the ruin of King John's Palace at Clarendon as an unsuitable subject, my unwitting guide then declared that he must now depart and with no invitation forthcoming for me to continue in his company, I was content to find my own way back to the Winterslow Hut. As I took one final look about the place a bright flash upon the horizon then caught my eye and I called out aloud; "Look there".

Mr Hazlitt stopped to observe me and then his silent gaze followed the direction of my outstretched arm. "There it is again." I stated "It is my spyglass. I am certain of it."

"Firstly it is pencils, then hats on tables and now spyglasses' upon distant hills, you are indeed a curious fellow Mr Chalk."

I had already embarked upon my direct course towards the glinting object and called back; "I have not the time to explain."

It was now Mr Hazlitt's turn to pursue me for I did not at first realise that curiosity had overwhelmed his desire for solitude. I had reached the floor of the valley when I had cause to start as Mr Hazlitt drew along side me. Between breathless pauses I then recounted the details of the gift of the spyglass and the witnessing of the same bright flash upon the distant long barrow that preceded the realisation of its loss. Mr Hazlitt appeared to enjoy this mystery and also the prospect of its resolution and he assisted in guiding our course for we no longer had sight of our distant goal. I was not prepared for such exertions and neither did we have between us a single drop of water and it was I that was soon perspiring greatly and lessening my pace as Mr William Hazlitt forged ahead. I was not to be left behind and determination soon brought us together again stride for stride. As we climbed the final ascent I could now see that our destination was an earthen encampment upon the crest of the hill and it was these distinct lines that had formed the crisp horizon visible from the ruined palace. The raised form of a Roman Road crossed our path, dormant under its blanket of turf and in a hundred more paces we bisected the dusty London Road, all the while with an eye upon the fortification ahead. I can inform you Sir that when we mounted the steep vallum of Figsbury Ring, for that is its name, there was no other person to be seen and twice now the pursuit of my phantom spyglass has been in vain. As I slumped down upon the grassy bank Mr William Hazlitt was unperturbed at my disappointment and suggested that the thrill of the chase was justification enough. Neither was I permitted to dwell over this further frustration as my companion was insistent that we made a circuit of the place.

"Come Mr Chalk, nature does not commiserate for the lark sings heartily in the heavens and neither is the small blue butterfly grief stricken by your loss. Let us walk some more."

There was not the width to walk two abreast upon the raised outer ring of the fortification and so I trailed behind my tireless companion and was soon to shed my disappointment for indeed there was beauty all around us to behold. Across the central expanse within the earthwork a carpet of yellow flowers dazzled in the sun and the once creamy blossom of a lone thorn bush was now bleeding pink in maturity. As we progressed on our circular course, Salisbury Cathedral was soon to reveal itself with its spire barely able to pierce the pale ridge beyond and Old Sarum could also be detected crouching below the horizon, such was the extent of our own elevation. Indeed Figsbury Ring had suffered no accident of placement by its ancient constructors for it commanded distant views in every direction. With Mr Hazlitt perhaps thirty paces ahead of me I was soon to notice that the path between us was a straight line and not the gentle curving arc that is associated with a circle. Now alert to this curiosity and five more paces on, Mr Hazlitt's direction altered perceptibly and it was as if the ring was not after all a true circle but instead comprised of many facets to make a round. Each facet of this narrow ridge was a straight line of perhaps thirty paces or more, a ditch dug straight, a straight bank also and how many of these sections were required to complete the whole? With this pleasing observation I then engaged in imagining the digging of this great entrenchment, not as a continuous and daunting endeavour but instead apportioned in short and manageable straight sections. I caught up with Mr Hazlitt to describe the part that he has played in assisting with the unravelling of this antiquarian conundrum. Without lessening his pace or turning his head Mr Hazlitt then gave no encouragement to my discovery.

"I am not a practical man Mr Chalk and this is surely a practical matter and whether it be done yesterday or many centuries ago I shall not consider it. Tell me it was done in the spirit of revolution and I shall be all ears but I propose that fear alone made this place."

With this rebuff I could only smile to myself and puzzle on what Mr Hazlitt meant by the "spirit of revolution".

At our first meeting Mr Hazlitt would not meet my eye and I thought him rude, yet today I have found a strange attraction to his company. He is not I believe a wealthy man and yet he has the luxury of a great mind in which to reside with its many rooms. I do not understand all of what he says yet there is a certainty to each word for it has a precision and a sharpness that has been honed by long and private consideration. Mrs Hazlitt had informed me earlier of her husband's dual occupation as an author and also a painter and yet I felt that the subject of poetry may also be embraced by this curious and most able minded gentleman. I had received short shrift upon my antiquarian observation and yet now as I trailed at the back of Mr William Hazlitt and had not his dark scowl to contend with, I found myself enquiring whether the making of poetry was also a "practical matter". I was quite prepared for a further haughty rebuff to this impertinence and continued with some trepidation.

"No," came the eventual reply and I at first thought this the end of the matter.

"No Mr Chalk, composing poetry is not ..a practical matter ..and I thank you for the kind return of my words ..like books, they suffer at the hands of the borrower with bindings scuffed and page corners turned over. I am not a poet but I have some association with that breed. They are assuredly not practical men."

Mr Hazlitt chuckled to himself as if reminded of some demonstration of great impracticality that confirmed this notion and then paused before reflecting that the poet Wordsworth would find this circuit ideal for the composition of poetry.

"I see him now going round and round and the continuity of his verse should suffer no interruption. The same arrangement would not do at all for Mr Coleridge for he is a very different animal."

I then asked my companion what would be Mr Coleridge's preference for I considered that these were indeed cast aside treasures on how our poets conjured their work from thin air and I was determined to retain them.

" Oh..give him instead a piece of uneven ground to tumble about on or a dense thicket through which to struggle and that would serve him well enough."

Mr Hazlitt then enquired as to my age and I informed him that I was now eighteen years old.

"I do not envy your intellect Mr Chalk but I would exchange our years for as we taste the pleasures of life the spirit evaporates. In youth our ideas are clothed and fed and pampered with these good and abundant spirits and we breathe thick and thoughtless happiness. I had the good fortune to make the acquaintance of poets whilst still enveloped in youth's slow waking dream and for that I shall always be thankful and yet it did not shape me to be a poet. You are ripe for poetry and the company of poets, question them about their..trade, do not ask me."

With three or more furious circuits of Figsbury Ring already to our name I wondered in desperation how many more Mr Hazlitt would now contemplate. With my lips cracking in the sun and a throat as dry as chalk, I wished for all the world to throw myself down upon the grassy slopes of this place and rest. In calm reflection as I write these words and sip cool water, I still do not know why I continued to compete so in this physical manner. Mr Hazlitt is perhaps ten or more years my senior and measure for measure I cannot match his brain but I had determined that I would not be defeated by this extraordinary gentleman's legs. I resented more and more his shape striding ahead of me as I stumbled meekly behind until I felt that I had not the strength to walk another step in pursuit. In my parched and deluded condition I wished to strike him down or leap upon his back to cease these endless revolutions and then I near walked into him for he had stopped to face me upon the narrow ridge.

"Walking alone is the path to all good thoughts Mr Chalk whether you be a poet, painter or pedestrian. I crave company in the city and solitude in the country and I am not for criticising hedgerows and black cattle, I simply wish to see my vague notions float like the down of thistle before the breeze. Once I begin I am elsewhere, in the grateful motion of walking with the blood doing what blood does around the body. I sense the beauty that envelops; the gate now an entrance to my thoughts; the bridge adjoins two estranged notions and the bramble tears at the skin but shall not disturb me from my meditations. Solvitur ambulando, Mr Chalk."

Our encircling of this ancient ring was now at an end for Mr Hazlitt trotted down the raised bank of the fortification and took a new direction towards the north where I was not required to follow. I slumped to the ground and watched his disappearing form and observed that he cast no shadow under a vertical sun. With his departure all possibilities then turned to vapour and I then became lost upon the path to lucid understanding.

How long I sat, crumpled amongst the folds of Figsbury Ring I do not know. In time I sought the shade of a thorn bush and observed the rabbits in their slow dismantling of the ancient embankment.

There exists within the centre of this fortification a large inner ditch and with no great accompanying bank, I then wondered that the spoil from this ditch was utilised to raise further the outer vallum? Mr Hazlitt is correct in referring to the construction of this place as a "practical matter" and I make no apology for my interest in such prosaic issues.

Rabbits have been at work here also upon this inner ring and I retrieved a bright white nodule of chalk and immediately sensed the dryness of it in my mouth as if this property had penetrated through my finger tips. This nodule bore all the marks of its extraction with deep scratches and claw marks where it had been ripped from beneath the turf by the industrious rabbit. As man builds, so will nature undo.

With no prospect of even a splash of water to quench my slating thirst I made my weary way back to the Winterslow

Hut. The busy London Road was too dusty to contemplate and I chose instead its quiet ancestor, the Roman Road, to return me to Winterslow. I encountered, upon the final ascent to the village, a modern deviation from the unerring straightness of the old road and a little sunken lane wound its way up between steep and chalky banks with tall trees providing welcome shade for toiling horses and parched Pedestrians. Before descending again to the London Road from the elevation of the village I sat for a while to look out upon the great expanse of open Plain that extended for as far as the eye could see beyond the Winterslow Hut. I had thus far only considered activities at the front of this place with the frustration of hopeful arrivals but I shall tomorrow explore this open tract of land.

Upon my leaden footed return to the Winterslow Hut I sought out the well and drank greedily from the pail before retiring to my room to cast myself upon the bed and I did not arise until dinner. As I complete these pages the light fades at the window and it is a golden glow that promises no interruption to this unseasonable heat.

You will gauge, my dear Uncle, that the curious Mr William Hazlitt has left his deep impression upon me. He has indeed provoked a great mixture of sensations of which awe and anger are most ably demonstrated as I read again my account of our strange excursion. Whilst in his company I believe that my mind is excited by a proximity that enables the transaction of a strange electricity. My thoughts then crackle with all these possibilities and yet upon his departure I was left a desiccated husk for this inspiration soon drained to the parched earth. There exists also an infuriation whilst in his company for his character does not bear this tremendous gift easily and his manner is barbed and ungenerous. I have not before felt the desire to strike any person however wronged I have been or how deserving the circumstance and yet today this sensation near overwhelmed me. I can make no excuse for this except that it may be a delusion caused by my exposure to the severity of the sun.

I wish you a good night my dear Uncle and I can inform you that I shall have not the slightest problem in sleeping soundly in my bed. Indeed it is those waking and waiting hours by which I suffer for I am not then deeply cosseted within my sweetest dream.

Your weary nephew
HENRY CHALK

My dear Uncle,

It is Old May Day today and I have learned that there is to be a single stick contest here at the Winterslow Hut. The winner shall receive a hat and three guineas and I have been informed by an excitable chambermaid that there shall be great crowds here this afternoon. Indeed at breakfast the tables are all taken and more visitors are expected upon the diligence from Salisbury. I know not what this single stick contest entails but I welcome the distraction. Mr Hazlitt has today one letter from London and so I must make my journey up the hill to Middle Winterslow.

It was with some dread that I knocked upon the Hazlitt's cottage door and I wished only to fulfil my self imposed duty and to then hastily depart. I was greeted by a wan faced Mrs Hazlitt dressed only in her night gown who then dashed to the parlour to make fearful retching noises, leaving me at the threshold with Mr Hazlitt's correspondence in hand. I looked up and down the street to judge whether there were any witnesses to this unseemly behaviour. In time I could detect Mrs Hazlitt's weak voice straining to make herself heard from the parlour; "Mr Chalk... Henry.. please excuse me..it is but a morningtime occurrence. I am not ailing."

A cart trundled by and the driver offered only a sly glance

in return to the raising of my hat.

The breathless voice from within explained that Mr Hazlitt was painting in the woods and in return I called out that there was to be a single stick contest at the Hut this afternoon, for I could think of little else to say.

Mrs Hazlitt then slowly emerged and excused herself for not making me more welcome and accepted Mr Hazlitt's letter. I raised my hat and was about to bid the pale faced Mrs Hazlitt a good morning when she reflected upon attending the same event at the Hut with her brother, Mr John Stoddart, perhaps five years before. There was then an awkward silence whilst I shuffled on the doorstep and Mrs Hazlitt shivered in the warm morning sun before sighing deeply;

"We would do well to participate in village life. They already think my husband a strange fellow, pacing about the place or nailing his canvas to a tree .. I shall see to it that we attend.. please excuse me .."

Mrs Hazlitt then rushed back into the cottage whilst I took the opportunity to depart and wondered how such a sickness is to be arrived at if one is not indeed ailing. At the garden party in Pembrokeshire, before my departure, I overheard Mrs Eliza Fenton in conversation with their good neighbour, Mrs Gough, whose daughter married Mr Edwards. In hushed tones Mrs Gough expressed her concerns; "Mrs Fenton, woman do suffer overly, for is not the labour itself trial enough without the early morning sickness?"

If you will excuse my tittle-tattle, how can this same

circumstance be possible for Mr and Mrs Hazlitt? They have been married for barely one week and nature surely dictates that such a situation cannot be arrived at in so short a time. You are correct Sir, if I may anticipate your frown for it is indeed none of my business.

I have prompted myself to direct my attention towards Pembrokeshire, and I should now write my long overdue letter of apology to Mr and Mrs Fenton.

*

I am again at my small table before the open window but the harsh sun has slipped to a warm and hazy dusk and after the festivities of the afternoon I can report that all is now quiet. I see that I had promised to write to Mr and Mrs Fenton but distraction and procrastination have again conspired to ruin this plan. I must first give you my account of the Old May Day celebrations for there ensued the most unexpected event and I know not, my dear Uncle, what you shall make of it. Bruised and bloodied I then explored the tract of land to the rear of Winterslow Hut and I can barely contain a great excitement at my discoveries there. I fear though that I must first suffer your disapproval at the description of my unseemly public display beside the London Road, outside the Winterslow Hut.

A finer day could not have been chosen for the Old May Day festivities for it was surely a welcome rest from the daily toil in the parlours, workshops, dairies and the fields about Winterslow. Ladies with baskets of ribbons and straw dolls sold their wares amongst the growing assembly whilst the tempting odour of freshly baked gingerbread wafted about the place. I purchased a pot of cider from a stall and at first sniffed at its acrid sharpness. After a sip I believed that I could not continue and then only by perseverance did it become tolerable. There was pleasure on the faces of these country people and as the cider crept about me in its warm embrace I soon felt as though I were a part of these proceedings and not just a stranger looking on. There were young men of my own age alive with expectation as pretty girls blushed at their mother's arm. The working elders mustered in twos and threes and had a word or two for the occasion as they sucked upon their long pipes;

"A proper druck o' volk Zimon."

"Ahh, n' Lanlard a wust var beer I zees."

Labourers seeking work remained stern faced and aloof amidst the frivolity, standing in silence with crook, pail or whip in hand to display their trade to each passing Farmer or his Steward. The landlord who had previously demonstrated a weary indifference to all that the busy London Road could offer now appeared full of good cheer at the success of the afternoon and slapped a large hand upon my back to make the cider leap from my pot. "Mr Chalk. Mr Chalk." Other guests and acquaintances received similar irreverential treatment with a litany of surnames and spilt ale or cider left in his wake as he made his way through the crowd. Having replenished my pot I then witnessed the most astonishing spectacle for I encountered two men each standing upon a chair and taking turns in making the most grotesque faces through a horse collar. The prize of a pound of tobacco was to be awarded to the creator of the most fiercesome countenance or indeed the visage devoid of all sense and understanding. The most versatile performers could achieve both these extremes and even extended their range to form subjects as diverse as a baboon or the elusive great bustard that I have yet to encounter upon the southern Plains of Wiltshire. The next contender had barely formed his features into "the spout of a jug" when he was jeered at by the assembled crowd for his efforts and this performance then ended abruptly as an egg hit him square in the face. It was at this moment of chaotic revelry that I spied Mr and Mrs Hazlitt and I made my way around the crowd to greet them. As they stood arm in arm viewing the curious spectacle of the "grinning match", as it is so called, they may have formed the perfect picture of newly weds enjoying their first excursion if it were not for Mr Hazlitt scowling and looking so ill at ease. Mrs Hazlitt had evidently recovered from her bout of sickness of this morning and Mr Hazlitt had a smudge of green paint upon his right ear. I heartily recommended the cider barrel for I had now fully overcome the initial strangeness of this drink. Mrs Hazlitt encouraged her husband to indulge whilst she spied an acquaintance and excused herself to leave me with Mr Hazlitt. He then muttered upon how there is a single character that is formed by the components of any crowd. As the next contorted face appeared through the horse collar Mr Hazlitt made a decree that we should all be awarded a prize to observe this exercise in deformity.

To assuage his unwillingness to enjoy the afternoon I fetched my companion a pot of cider at which he sniffed suspiciously whilst children ran about his feet attempting to capture a greased piglet.

There was a distinction between the local revellers and those who had travelled some distance with only the main event in mind. At first I believed that any fool could wield a club in the single stick contest but these are fellows who know their sport and are accompanied by a throng of supporters. At the announcement of the first stick battle the thrust of interest was palpable with the well dressed pushing to the fore whilst the countrymen were made to give way. Raised voices shouted the odds with wagers struck and of a sudden wide eyed expectation had replaced the rustic hilarity of the afternoon. I followed Mr Hazlitt into the thick of the circle for he was as keen as any to witness the first crunching blows. The stick is a yard of heavy ash-wood with an enclosed basket hilt around the handle giving the appearance of a brutish sword. The combatants are placed near together and all strikes are delivered with a whipping motion from a high guard. The left hand must grip a scarf tied loosely around the thigh and this barely enables the forearm to protect the face with elbow raised. Blows are confined to the head and upper body and none may strike to the back of the head. A winner is determined by the drawing of a bead of blood from the opponent's head that must measure greater than one inch in length as declared by the judge of the competition. These are indeed the rules as best I can comprehend them and I confess that I have not before witnessed anything so harmful and yet so strangely compelling. The crowd roars in unison as blows are struck and I found myself adjoining this single voice under a sweltering sun. The bout appears endless as sticks clash, flesh is welted and bruises grow to a slippery redness under a sheen of sweat. Of a sudden the knowing crowd sensed blood and roared their man to victory, although I could discern no advantage to either party but one fellow was soon sprawling in the dust and we surged forward to gain a view of the gashed forehead to determine that the contest was over. No measurement was required of the judge for the white shirt of the vanquished contestant was soon blood soaked as he was escorted away by his men. The victor was hailed with his arm raised in triumph to which he looked bemused as if unaware of his contribution to the proceedings. Wagers were settled and cider pots were laced with strong rum in celebration. Mr Hazlitt rubbed his hands together in anticipation of the next bout and upon the London road a party of volunteers were cheered as they passed by on their way to Salisbury. The perspiring marchers to the rear of the group gestured to the onlookers for drinks and hung out their tongues as they observed the festivities at the Winterslow Hut. Cider was quickly slopped into pots and conveyed by eager boys and girls to quench the thirst of these local protectors of our sovereignty. Those to the fore of the marching party faltered at this unfairness until the Captain rode back to call a halt to this unscheduled provision. We established that these were the Avon and Bourne and Blacklands volunteers returning from a fortnight's duty at Winchester and their unbending Captain was Sir Richard Malet. Amongst the throng more pots were raised and toasts proposed "To King and Country" and "The brave men of England". The despicable tyrant Napoleon Bonaparte was then called any number of names and in this tumult of English loving and French hating I found myself boasting of my own part in the apprehension of a dangerous Frenchman only two days previously. As you will know my Dear Uncle from my own account that this is an untruth, indeed a lie and yet in this fervour I puffed out my chest and praise for my actions was swiftly forthcoming from those hot and swaying men around me and was soon broadcast loudly for all to hear. In no time I was tossed aloft to cries of "Hip, Hip, Hurrah" and so of a sudden from my idle falsehood I had become at once a hero and more toasts were proposed. Upon the instant that my feet returned to the ground I was met by a look of fury and spitting hostility from Mr William Hazlitt. "You are no better than these red faced fools, indeed much worse. I cannot abide such displays of ignorant pride."

In the lurching crowd Mr Hazlitt was forced hard up against me and continued his hissing tirade; "Hard words and hard blows are all that an Englishman can understand and his brain is no more than soft-boiled meat." I then stumbled back in the shifting tide of the swelling crowd and this motion was construed as a push by one nearby who had witnessed Mr Hazlitt's venomous intent towards me. Mr Hazlitt was then confronted and told that if there was a grievance between ourselves then it should be fairly resolved. This opportunity then spread about the crowd like a summer heath fire and our hats and jackets were quickly stripped away and the sticks that were soon to be employed in the next bout were thrust into our hands. Scarves were sought and hastily applied to tether our left wrists in the correct manner. A deal of pushing back and calling out soon formed space enough for this impromptu combat, a judge was self appointed and in the blink of an opportunity odds were taken. These sudden and alarming circumstances had not served to temper Mr William Hazlitt's fury and the cries of "Hero" were still ringing loudly in my ears and I had consumed enough of the cider barrel to wallow in this unfounded praise. Mr Hazlitt was goaded into making the first thrust forward and our sticks cracked together as I made a successful defence of my skull. The high forehead of my opponent made an ample target and yet each lunge forward was repelled by nimble stick work and the crowd offered their own solution to this empasse. "Break 'is arm. Get 'im in the ribs."

I think back now to the blur of this horror, as the crowd snarled about us and that we were both fully intent on causing untold damage to one another when only moments before I had considered Mr Hazlitt my companion. I still do not know the true cause of his anger towards me save for my shameful boasting for which I fully deserved any sound beating. I can only judge that Mr Hazlitt holds a sympathy for England's greatest foe as I recall yesterday the encircling of Figsbury Ring and Mr Hazlitt's dismissal of my proposal as to how such a place was constructed. He then made a remark which I did not at that time comprehend; "Tell me it was done in the spirit of Revolution and I shall be all ears.."

Does he indeed believe that "Le Terror" was a just solution to the tradition of order and aristocracy for I have heard that such Englishmen exist and would perhaps wish the guillotine to be erected upon Hyde Park Corner?

As our sticks reigned down upon one another, in my opponents mind, perhaps it was I that represented the ignorance of the British people? Was I not the face, forehead and single character of a crowd of misguided Englishmen who did not grasp the glorious purpose of the revolution or the actions of its child, Napoleon Bonaparte? Mr William Hazlitt was an older, stronger and angrier man than I and was to eventually gain the upper hand and drive me back for all the stout defence that I could muster. Blows struck my forearm and shoulder and in this miniature battle our great Nation was about to suffer the ultimate assault and all freedom would soon be lost if it were not for the timely intervention of Mrs Hazlitt.

"WILLIAM!"

Mrs Sarah Hazlitt forced her way between the human wall that surrounded us and entering the ring grasped the stick from her husband's hand. "William, what on earth..and Mr Chalk?"

The crowd protested as one at this interruption but the severity of Mrs Hazlitt's ejection of her husband from the proceedings caused sufficient mocking laughter and ribald comment to temporarily quell the lust for blood. Attention quickly turned to the real competition and I was left a forgotten hero to collect my hat and coat from amongst the dust before quietly retreating with shirt torn and an arm that has become a throbbing reminder of my stupidity. What a fool I have been to be caught up and carried along in the frenzy of a drunken crowd with all good sense abandoned. What do you think of me now my dear Uncle?

The great exertion and the blows of the single stick contest had somehow dispelled the effects of the cider but a raging thirst required a quart or more of water at the well. To rid myself of the roars, cheers and mirth of the Old May Day festivities I then stumbled along without aim upon the barren Plain to the rear of the Winterslow Hut. I was at first drawn to a great barrow that would surely be worthy of the attentions of Mr William Cunnington's men for it appeared complete and unviolated by the tomb robber. Indeed there were a number of the same clustered about and I fancied that I should seek a pick and a spade and become barrow mad in the conduct of my own investigation. As I form these words upon the page in calm contemplation before an unwavering flame, I wonder at the creation of these barrow clusters for they are to be encountered at every turn across the open Plains of Wiltshire. The setting about Stonehenge is indeed a place for a conspicuous burial in the manner that Westminster Abbey is a place for a fine tomb and worthy neighbours. We cannot all be housed in Westminster Abbey nor our ancient ancestors within the shadow of Stonehenge and so there must be modest churches and empty Plains in which to reside upon our demise. It is a mistake to think on empty Plains for were there not planted fields, tended herds, villages, paths, festivities and a place where the earth is heaped upon the passing generations? In the neighbourhood about the Winterslow Hut, before the construction of a Hut, the building of a road or even the thought of a Capital City, a grand barrow of white chalk was once raised to shine brightly in the sun. The deceased was surely a wealthy chief and had possessions, of which a portion accompanied him to his chalky eternity, but is it not the barrow itself that speaks loudly of possession? To the ancient stranger who once traversed these Plains this vast beacon of whiteness warned of occupation and a people now prospering in life and death with more tombs on the way.

I do not believe that I had any such thoughts in my head as I sat upon the largest of these barrows for I could still hear the distant drifting cheers of a drunken crowd and so set off further into the Plain until these sounds no longer troubled my senses.

It is a Plain with a plethora of dark stunted bushes and a grass carpet already pale and parched by the drying sun but it is by no means a plain Plain for it is enamelled by the prettiest of small flowers. There is a shifting decoration also in the brightness of the day as butterflies alight and depart upon a silent whim whilst the open sky is filled with sparkling song. The originator of this ethereal music is I believe the lark and it has accompanied me throughout my short journey in South Wiltshire. Under my feet I found areas where the steady green sward was interrupted by a rash of bumps or small hillocks and on close inspection I established that these are caused by the industrious ant. I hopped about from hump to hump as I recalled Mr Hazlitt's observations on how Mr Coleridge preferred uneven ground upon which to compose his verse. Alas no poetry was forthcoming and instead I soon found myself sprawling amongst the ants. I chose instead a dusty track to follow and passed by flocks of the ubiquitous Wiltshire sheep whose appetite for grass appears insatiable and I willed that they might break with this tradition to perform a jig or muster into lines and curves to spell giant words and thereby astound mankind. Try as I might, I could detect no such behaviour and trod carefully least I wakened a shepherd who lay peacefully in the shade of a small bush with his cider flask laying uncorked and empty by his side. After a lifetime of tending to these predicable creatures it is indeed fortunate that he has not missed such theatrics through daylight slumber.

With no water to satiate my thirst I curtailed my progress towards the centre of this Plain and instead took a track that enabled me to walk with the sun at my back and in time turned again to direct me back towards the London Road. My mind was vacant and I kept it so least I should dwell upon my folly with Mr William Hazlitt and I believe that I should have missed altogether a most remarkable discovery if it were not for the interruption of a stranger.

I had paused to observe a small herd of deer that were in turn observing my progress when of a sudden the quietness of this Plain exploded and sent me headlong into the shelter of a grassy hollow. With my ears still numb from this assault I peered out from this sanctuary to establish the cause of such thunder and spied a tall Gentleman with a large and smouldering gun in the crook of his arm standing not ten paces away. His face was screwed up with the effort of peering into the distance as if confronted by a thick fog and he then ambled forward to squint at who was to blame for the disturbance of his prey and an opportunity lost.

"A p.p.p..pox on you sir… now the b.b.b..bustards have f.f..flown to who knows where. A p.p.p..pox I say."

I stood up in my hole to confront this Hunter who appeared keen to apportion his faltering blame upon me and I informed him that I had witnessed nothing in that same direction but a herd of deer.

"F.f.f..fiddle f.f.f..faddle Sir, there were a half d..d..d.. dozen or more at my m..mercy, d..d..d*mn your eyes."

I felt a great temptation to correct this grumbling gentleman that it was his own eyes that were beyond salvation and that

I would indeed take my pleasure in disturbing his intentions if it would spare the elusive great bustard from its fate. I believe however that the deer were no more in danger than the bustard from the effects of this inept hunter's murderous tube and with his departure I was left in my hollow to poke at two deaf ears.

I now thank this Hermes of the Plains for without my near perforation by a charge of swan shot I should have passed on my vacant way and returned in near walking slumber to the Winterslow Hut. Indeed our encounter was most fortuitous for once I had stepped from my grassy hollow I then spied that the ground all about was littered with flint pieces formed in the manner that occurs only by human intervention. I have before described, my dear Uncle, the signs of such manipulation and they were plain to see on every piece and yet these fragments were broad and often very long. I sat back down to wonder upon this occurrence and picked up two large pieces that had been made white by their long exposure to the elements and upon tapping them together they chimed like the best porcelain. I then shattered another segment by pounding it with a large nodule and revealed within the rich darkness of the most perfect flint. Such profligacy could only occur at an abundant source of this material and I looked again at my grassy hollow and nearby there were similar depressions. Amongst this pock marked ground I found also nests of blue-grey gunflint waste. There is no question of the longevity of the older industry for the whiteness of the larger flint pieces is absolute whilst the recent gunflint detritus is barely clouded over by comparison.

My thirst and lethargy in the hot sun melted with the notion that perhaps these hollows were once holes in the ground from which this excellent flint was extracted and I leapt up and ran from one to the next until I lost count of their number. At the base of one such hollow I picked up a bar of white flint that I gauge measures perhaps ten inches in length and is roughly hewn but I hold no doubt that its maker had every intention of forming a large axe for one end is bevelled to make a cutting edge. I have it upon the table before me and it is a crude and unfinished tool and was perhaps discarded for a more perfect piece of flint but I care not about its imperfections for it speaks loudly of an ancient industry that once existed upon this Plain.

I shall now hasten to my bed as all theory must be proven by examination and I will rise at first light to request the loan of a pick and a spade from the blacksmith. Sir, before my discovery here behind the Winterslow Hut, I can admit to vain hope above firm belief. I am bruised but my faith in "A Tour in Search of Flint" has been restored.

Your impetuous nephew
HENRY CHALK

MY DEAR UNCLE,

I can now understand well enough from the blisters upon my hands the stoic role played by Mr William Cunnington's two barrow diggers, Steven and John Parker. To arrive at noon to view the progress of a morning's toil is the way of the gentleman antiquary. To mix with the soil and impart one's own blood to the venture is heroic but foolhardy.

You will be impatient to learn of my progress thus far and I now realise that this is no short exploration beneath the turf. I began in a fury by hacking away at the grass and soil and then spread it about this way and that with no order. I have since exhausted myself and by necessity I dig and rest a while and drink greedily from my water pail. There has been some encouragement in the copious shards of white flint that I have uncovered and I have learnt to inspect each spadeful and ensure some order to the growing spoil heap.

I must retrace my steps as to my choice of grassy hollow for as I have indicated this ground is pock-marked by these depressions and I cannot examine them all. I found again the position where I retrieved the long rough flint axe for I believe it to be a good omen as to what may lie beneath the soil. These hollows vary also in their breadth and my chosen pit is perhaps smaller than many and therefore easier for a sole excavator who has smooth hands and muscles unused to hard labour. It has been sheltered from the sun to some small degree by a clump of these stunted bushes which also makes a screen to prying eyes for I am uncertain of the consequences of my making a large hole upon this ground. In this heat the ink dries quickly upon the page for the sun has now climbed above the stunted bushes to blaze upon the fresh white chalk. You will see how my hand shakes with the effects of this labour but continue I must.

*

Toil frees the mind and the mind can drift to strange places whilst the body is left behind to work like a machine upon the earth.

I have considered Mr William Hazlitt at length for my bruised and aching shoulder is a persistent reminder of that gentleman but I shall not bear him any ill will. I believe that I have learned much in his presence and also by the folly of our single stick encounter. You will recall that Colonel Boyle, some days ago at the Woodyates Inn, urged me to be both brave and bold in life. Being brave is not just pretending to be brave or being seen to be brave in the eyes of others. Bravery is I believe a boldness in one's convictions and being brave enough to defend them. For all that I do not understand Mr Hazlitt's convictions, he does not for one moment consider the consequences of these convictions nor does he stint in their defence. I do not believe that he would permit our friendship, such as it was, to prosper further for I sense that his nature is unforgiving and without compromise. After all that has passed then perhaps I should also cast him adrift as a companion and yet I feel a great reluctance to do so for I shall treasure the moments that I spent in his company. Whilst striding in his wake there was much to stimulate the mind and I sensed that a greater understanding was waiting just beyond the brow of the next hill if only I could keep pace with this extraordinary gentleman. I can now recall a fraction of our one sided conversations and Mr Hazlitt's well considered thoughts were akin to pouring out a rich cream to quench a raging thirst and I could consume but very little. Consider if you will, my dear Uncle, this savoured moment of consolation from Mr William Hazlitt; "One truth discovered, one pang of regret at not being able to discuss it, is better than all the fluency and flippancy in the world".

*

I am learning as I go and I believe that I must devise some means to make a record of my progress. I require a length of string along which a number of measured knots may be tied. I must again visit the blacksmith for I shall also require another pail to haul the spoil from the deepening excavation. The blacksmith is a man of few words and I know not what he thinks of each new request.

*

Sir, I now hold a fear within me that this was indeed not a pit for the abstraction of flint. What if it were a pit dwelling and, by their close proximity, a village of similar dwellings? There is no question that flint abounds here but is not this fashioned flint a mere residue of ancient occupation? I have become of a sudden made weary by this notion and so laid down my tools in despair.

This is a circumstance where I must consider what Mr William Cunnington would advise if he were here. I believe that he would inform me kindly that my yearning for a source of the best quality flint will not change one jot the result of my excavation. I cannot make a silk purse from a sow's ear. Will not the discovery of so many pit dwellings cast a great light upon the habits of our ancient ancestors? We have not before learnt where the carpenter, the ploughman, or the cow-herd lived in an age when metal was unknown. I also take solace in Mr Richard Fenton's bold statement that "We speak from facts not theory" for I believe that it is the gathering of small facts that will one day elevate a gentleman's pastime to a noble science. Who is to say that each spadeful of these tiny snail shells that lay buried amidst this soil is not worthy of record for I have today cast a great many upon the spoil heap with little thought until now?

*

I have just retrieved a fine flint celt of perhaps six inches in length and also a number of worn sections of deer antler. The chalk rubble is packed tight toward the edges of the pit but I have found it easier to disturb toward the middle. I have now reached a depth of four feet by my estimation and do not know whether to be encouraged or discouraged by the discovery of a seam of inferior flint. It appears that the ancient excavators have taken little heed of it for I can see no signs of it being prized out from the original side of the pit. It is however a confirmation that flint, in its natural condition, exists in these horizontal seams.

The snakecatcher's hat is sodden but I dare not remove it for it is my only defence against the burning sun. My dear Uncle I am exhausted. There is a small bird that occupies these dark stunted bushes and it has a call like the chinking together of two flint pieces. I have made it hop closer to investigate as I tap the flint celt upon another nodule and it now perches upon my water pail. Chink, chink, chink.

A curious event has just occurred. Whilst I struggled to keep my eyes from closing I have seen figures shimmering in the sun with their skin a ghostly white. These spectres gathered around the chalk spoil and I could smell their odour. An old man squatted down at the edge of the pit and I could hear voices straining, singing, coughing and the chink, chink, chink of flint upon flint. I strained to view again this ethereal scene but the white ghosts are turned to sheep and the old man is now a shepherd leant upon his crook as he observes my excavation. We did not speak and the shepherd and his flock have now drifted beyond the stunted bushes. I believe that I am soon to be driven mad by this accursed sun.

*

It was all I could do to drag these aching bones from a comfortable bed to resume this penance to my own curiosity.

I must also record that the day is Sunday. These hands are no longer my own for they will not do as I request and have suffered greatly by this labour but I dearly wish to conclude my excavation before the arrival of Mr Robert Foster tomorrow. Last evening I stowed the pick and spade beneath a bush and today I have slopped across the Plain with two pails of water reasoning that a great deal would spill forth. Water is a heavy burden to transport but I now have one full pail for two halves make a whole and indeed I am now curious as to how the ancient peoples who once occupied this Plain availed themselves of water. Is not the digging of wells the preserve of our more recent ancestors? In the heart of winter I understand that there are fresh springs that emerge from the ground near the Hut and rainwater may also be caught and preserved. In the dry barren months then water must be transported across some distance, perhaps from the river valley to the north of this Plain. I cannot believe that an ancient water carrier would be so profligate as to lose half of what they started out with and so some sealed vessel would be preferable to an open pail.

*

I have obtained a depth of six feet but I realise that I must now remove a larger volume of material to create a working platform. Without this reorganisation my tapered shaft is not sufficiently wide enough to swing the pick and as I am not some chalk burrowing animal that can penetrate the earth with its claws I must therefore broaden the aperture of this

hole. This is demoralising work for the already excavated
sections soon fill with this fresh spoil to create the antithesis
of progress.

*

I have been spared further torment for the blacksmith has
unexpectedly arrived at my excavation and demanded the
return of the pick and spade.

"Tis Zundee."

I obediently handed back the tools and then watched his
retreating figure whilst standing upon my freshly constructed
ledge of chalk with my head just able to peer out from the
hole. I felt too exhausted to resist or even question this
blunt request. Hitherto I have found the Blacksmith silently
obliging and yet today his conviction has demanded that he
should cause a cessation to my labours. So be it.

*

I am now returned to the Winterslow Hut and I shall not now
complete my exploration before the arrival of Robert Foster
tomorrow. I believe that I have wrecked my body and covered
myself with chalkdust, all to no purpose. The chambermaid
has just departed and I now know all that is to be known
about the other guests and how the doctor who arrived last
evening was taken ill but did not wish to cause any trouble
by his condition. Neither did he wish to summon a doctor for
he is a doctor and he insists that the drapes are kept drawn
at all times to keep out the sun. The doctor is a very polite
gentleman and he wished to know who was presently residing

at the Inn for any duration. As the chambermaid disturbed the fine white dust that has settled upon the contents of my room and then pulled my bed about she continued with her chatter and I believe that by her speech she is not a Wiltshire girl; "..and I told 'im that there was you, young Master Chalk, and Mr and Mrs Saunders who have bin 'ere since I don't know when and Mr James who is moving to London now that 'is Mother has passed away God rest 'er soul. Then the Doctor says if it i'nt too much trouble could 'ee be moved to a quiet room cos the noise from the kitchen below disturbs 'is sleep and 'e gives me a shillin' to talk to the landlord. 'Ee's now across the 'all from you Master Chalk and 'e wishes to keep the door open fer the air but 'e dun't look well, no 'e dun't look well at all Master Chalk."

To be listed amongst the residents of the Winterslow Hut has only served to increase my gloom and I must now flee this place for the remainder of the day. I shall further explore this Plain and perhaps encounter a subject suitable for the pencil.

*

The day has passed well enough but upon my return to the Winterslow Hut I then stopped to again observe my excavation. I embarked upon a further drawing and in that time an ever deepening shadow settled upon the pit. It is as if by the digging of this pit I have disturbed something that lay buried deep within me and from this white hole in the ground a black and restless spirit has emerged to haunt my thoughts and unsettle my senses. I cannot now dispel the memory of my father's fury upon witnessing me at play amongst the chalk spoil during the digging of the great well in the yard at Chalk's brewery in Southwark. Sir, I have written before of this occasion and the many long months of excavation endured by the well diggers employed to the task. With each passing week my father would stare down into the yard whilst wringing his hands and he then would curse me for suggesting the venture in the first place. One afternoon I watched from my desk as the extracted spoil changed from a pale clay slop to bright white lumps of chalk and of a sudden this brightness made the yard an exceedingly dull place. I could not contain my fascination and ran to inspect this magical white material caring not that my hands, clothes and boots all turned white in an instant. It was at this same moment that my father, your brother, returned to the brewery with the gentleman from the bank to observe the progress of this deepening investment. Whilst my father trembled with silent rage the representative from the bank shook his head at my antics and uttered words that I shall never forget: "In name and nature, Master Chalk". With the departure of the bank official no effort was spared in my punishment with the lesson that I must be fixed in my ambition to one day be the owner of a fine brewery and not a simple labourer. From that day on my father only addressed me upon matters of business where my clerical duties demanded his attention. Even the eventual success of the well did little to alleviate his mood and I was to dread each evening as we sat down at the table to eat our dinner in silence. I came to believe that my presence was a constant reminder of everything bad that had passed his way. My mother had suffered greatly at my birth and yet she did in time recover only to succumb at the birth of my sister. I stood at her bedside and watched as she grew so very pale until all life faded from her beautiful face. My sister Elizabeth lived but two weeks when she also passed from this world. I could not understand how first the loss of my mother could occur and then that of my most delicate sister Elizabeth. My father would not speak of it and for many years I believed that they had both died of a paleness to the skin. Should I ever encounter a person with a pale face then I would stand and stare to wonder if they to would soon also pass away. You will recall Sir, my conversation last autumn with Mr Richard Fenton on the subject of the losing of love and the affliction of a broken heart. Mr Fenton's good friend Sir Richard Colt Hoare lost his own wife Hester in childbirth some twenty years before and he now seeks distraction in the recording of the antiquities of Wiltshire. In the words of Mr Fenton; "Sir Richard lives and he smiles and sometimes he will laugh but only when his heart ceases to beat will it also cease to ache." I now believe that my father was so deeply in love with my mother that he could never recover from her passing. In my growing years I missed her dearly but could not comprehend this unseen world of love and loss until I met Miss Sarah Foster and sensed the stirring within my own heart. As I write these words and suffer these thoughts my tears mix with the all pervading chalk dust and dry quickly upon the cheek. There is much that has been extracted from this hole in the Plain for it appears that I have also encountered a rich seam of despair. I must now finally commit the circumstances of my father's death to the page. Sir, you did not attend your own brother's funeral and I can only believe that the cause of your absence was the belief held by some that his death was caused by self-murder. The Coroner ruled that a tragic accident had occurred for a verdict of self murder would demand that lunacy was recorded as the cause. I could not bring myself to believe such a thing. How could I think that my own father would chose to leave me alone in this world? It is only now that I am grown a little and have been shown that love is all conquering and how it can break the heart of even the strongest of men that I am thrown into doubt. In truth I do not know what occurred that evening and can only churn over again my own account of it which brings little solace. I do not believe that anything new may be gathered from a further trampling of these few facts that have become the threadbare carpet of my own soul such has been the pacing up and down upon it. I shall nevertheless continue even as my spirit sinks lower with each written word. There was a caller at the door before dinner with a note delivered to my father. I then heard a loud and pained exclamation from the study and so presumed that the note had contained ill and unwelcome news. I had been reading before dinner in the drawing room with only a wall to divide us and so could not fail to hear my father's raised voice. I have tried so often to recall the exact words uttered but I was so truly engrossed in the tale of Robinson Crusoe that my attention was late in arriving. I then listened intently to the ensuing silence and even wondered whether anything had actually occurred at all. The note was never retrieved and it may have contributed nothing to his silence at dinner or the sudden pushing back of the chair to leave his plate untouched. Indeed the outburst from the study was the last sound that I ever heard from my father's lips for he left the table, the dining room and the house with no excuse or explanation.

I am ashamed to think that I cared little for his departure only that a heavy cloud had been lifted from the house. I even retrieved my book from the drawing room and continued to read through the remainder of the meal whilst defiantly flicking over each fresh page. Sir, I had retired to my bed by the time that I received the dreadful news of my father's death and a chill runs through me now as I recall being shaken from my slumber. As I rubbed at my eyes I could not comprehend the great anxiety in the voice of our housekeeper Mrs Harrison and her insistence that I should accompany her to the drawing room. I even became angered at her reticence in not explaining why my sleep should be disturbed. The solemn faces that greeted me in the drawing room were sufficient to quell my anger and soon made me sober from the effects of interrupted sleep.

I was requested to sit down before a standing Mr Hooper and Mr Gerrity from the brewery and also a large Constable.

Mr Hooper spoke first and I recall observing his ashen face but I do not recall what was said until I heard the words:

"…Master Chalk, your father is dead."

My gaze became locked upon the actions of the Constable as he held onto his hat and rotated it between large and nervous fingers. The statement was then repeated and I could hear the sobbing of the housekeeper out in the hallway. Finally I believe I said "Yes", least they repeated the statement over and over again. This grim visitation then slowly divulged the circumstances of my father's death and how he was crushed beneath a carriage off Fleet Street. The Coroner's books must be filled with the details of such needless deaths. Fallen from carriages, fallen from horses, trampled by horses, crushed by the wheels of carriages. It is indeed a prosaic litany and a waste of life. Stifled by the awkwardness of these three late visitors I began to pace the room and then asked whether I could offer them a glass of something to which they all declined. Having delivered their news I then wondered how long they intended to stay for I could find no words or display any expected emotion.

Finally after clearing his throat the Constable asked whether I had any notion of why my father would be abroad so late in the evening. I recalled the delivery of a note before dinner and also my father's outburst and I then described his sudden departure from the house. The three men then glanced at one another before the Constable continued; "We believes Master Chalk, Sir, that your good father wus robbed as he expired in the street."

This announcement became the blow to cut me down, to make me sink to the floor, for with these words came the image of the final moments of my father's life. The three grim faced men were finally able to assist me in my grief, moving swiftly to see me to a chair with a relief upon their faces as they spoke generous words of consolation and deep sympathy.

It transpires that before the driver of the carriage could halt and return to attend to my father, a figure was observed crouching over his crushed body. This wretched thief then departed for no money nor his old fob watch was found upon my father. Indeed there was no means by which to place a name upon this poor soul until the body was carried to the Black Lion Inn nearby. By good fortune the old landlord did recognise my father for they had conducted business together when my father was a young collecting clerk who visited regularly to dip the barrels. I think again of my father's last moments and that act of cold robbery as he drew his final breath upon this earth. With my pen now faltering above the page the evening stage has just clattered into the yard below to disturb my painful reverie. The night is warm with the candle's flame so perfectly preserved before an open window and yet the door to my room has now opened of its own accord as if by a sudden draught of frozen air. My neck prickles and I must investigate further this strange and inopportune occurrence.

I do not know how to describe what happened next but I must, and in good order to, for it is a short tale with a fine

surprise at the end of it. Upon creeping to the open door I
then held aloft my candle to look up and down the hallway
and found no persons to east nor west. The door to the room
across the hall had earlier in the evening been left ajar as
instructed by the ailing doctor but it was now fully opened. I
moved across the hall to stand in this doorway and strained
my ears but could hear nothing but the beating of my own
heart. I now feared for the life of the poorly doctor but I was
held in stasis by some unknown force and could not proceed.
At that same moment the candle then spat and puffed itself
out to leave me in complete darkness. Sir, I then became
gripped by a certainty that there was indeed something
familiar within that room, a stirring of a memory or a sense
from my childhood. Of a sudden my orientation is lost and I
am returned to a time when our house in Southwark was not
a place of sadness or secrets but instead held my mother's
presence and her laughter. It was a time when you, My dear
Uncle, would arrive and demand that I fetch my toy soldiers
so that we might make a battle upon the floor. What could
possibly be the connection between these two places so far
apart in years and distance other than by the electricity of
my own thoughts? Upon writing these words I now recall the
terror of my childhood encounter with a dark and beckoning
room upon the top floor of our house. I believed that I had
heard noises from within and knew not where my mother was.
As I wavered timidly upon the threshold it was you my Dear
Uncle that emerged from the darkness to make me start so

and caused me to flee back down the stairs. You then located me amongst the skirts of kindly Mrs West in the kitchen and suggested that we should at once visit the Port of London and so we departed soon after. To a boy of seven years the sight of such giant ships teaming with sailors and a great dancing bear upon the dock became at once a romantic world of which to dream. Indeed this was to be my last association with you Sir for I cannot recall that you again visited our house.

To return to the curious and unsettling instance that has just occurred here at the Winterslow hut, I then heard a voice in the darkness and recognised it as my own; "Sir, are you ailing? Has your condition worsened?" I could hear no response and yet by the merest draught that betrays slow movement, I felt a presence so close that I might reach out and touch another person. Into this black void of mystery and the stirring of recognition came other voices and a flickering light from along the hallway. Boots appeared with a lamp to illuminate the scene and I could now witness my frozen position at the door to the doctor's room. "Mr Chalk, zur...?"

The person accompanying boots now stepped into the light and we studied one another before this gentleman then held out his hand; "Mr Robert Foster at your service, I am delighted to finally make your acquaintance Mr Chalk." All dark thoughts were dispelled by these words and by the warm and smiling countenance of Mr Robert Foster. Before I could alert boots to my concerns regarding the ailing doctor, the door to the doctor's room then slammed shut as if by some petulant hand. I know not what occurred before the arrival of boots and Robert Foster other than my black thoughts had summoned up some strange association that I cannot comprehend. I shall not dwell upon it for across the room from me sits Robert Foster, now attending to his own correspondence, and I cannot keep a smile from my face by his presence here at the Winterslow Hut. By good fortune Robert was able to depart from London sooner than expected and his sudden arrival has caused me great excitement. We have talked much already like two dear childhood friends or indeed brothers that have been estranged by distance and are now reunited. I am so deeply overwhelmed for I have not before known such close and familiar friendship. I have no secrets from Robert Foster for he has read aloud my correspondence to his beloved sister Sarah and by his own hand has committed to ink her every word in reply.

I believe that Robert has now completed his own correspondence and so I shall now bid you a goodnight my dear Uncle for there is much more that I wish to hear and to then hear again.

Your faithful nephew
HENRY CHALK

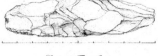

Scale of Ten Inches

Winterslow Hut

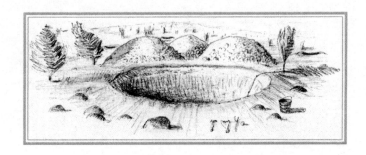

The Flint Pit

Floorstone (from the base of the flint pit)

MY DEAR UNCLE,

Mr Robert Foster and I both awoke in our chairs this morning such was the confabulation that went on long into the night. Robert opened his eyes to find me studying his face in the early morning light as I sought for a duplication of Sarah's features. He then obliged by displaying his profile.

"I am a Foster and have the pretty Foster nose. Pray Henry please can you explain why this room and indeed your own face is coated with white powder. Sir, you have been embalmed, observe yourself in the mirror. I thought you a spectral figure upon the landing last evening and worthy of a turn at Hamlet's Ghost."

Upon inspection my face was as described but the scouring by last evening's tears had spoiled this stage paint. I ensured Robert that I was indeed very much alive and was obliged to explain the circumstances of my quest for a source of the best quality flint. Robert listened patiently and then sighed deeply: "Henry Chalk, why am I not very much surprised by this news? I require breakfast."

Hot water was sought and upon the completion of our repast I then asked Mr Robert Foster of his plans for the day.

"Plans, Mr Chalk? Plans? Am I to be excluded from your antiquarian investigation?"

I explained that I did not consider for one instant that he should sully his clothes in this way but meant rather that I may join him in a trip to Salisbury as befits a visiting tourist. Robert pondered upon this proposition for a moment and then stated that all the talk in London had been of the famous and magnificent "White hole of Winterslow" and he was determined to see it for himself.

I now recognise raillery as a consequence of spending time in the company of Mr John Fenton and so was able to feign surprise. "I have attempted great discretion by my excavation Mr Foster..but sadly..the blacksmith has informed the shepherd and now..well..you know how it is ?"

"Exactly Henry.." concluded Robert ".. and now ..all London knows about it."

I then asked in all sincerity whether Robert wished to assist with the digging of the pit to which he concurred wholeheartedly. He has also volunteered to approach the blacksmith on my behalf to request the further use of the pick and the spade once we depart the Winterslow Hut. Today there is a heaviness in the air and I fear that work in the pit will be hard toil indeed.

With Robert soon to return home to Somerset, it is with a glad heart that I am able to recommence my correspondence to Miss Sarah Foster and so the dreadful hiatus shall come to an end. Indeed I have not forgotten the glimpse of that mislaid letter from one "Percy Bysshe" to the young lady of Ferne House for it has displayed how notions of love must be addressed. There must exist a dangerous fervour and a world in upheaval for thoughts of love cannot thrive in a safe and cosseted place. There shall be tumult and dreadful images as if we are clinging to flotsam upon a dark and boiling ocean or fleeing the burning wrath of a volcano. I believe that it makes my own past rhetoric to Sarah a calm and placid sea with not a wisp of wind and no prospect of a tempest upon the horizon.

*

Even with all our good organisation the morning was well in advance before we finally set out upon the Plain. We could hear the distant toll of a solitary bell as Robert went in search of the blacksmith whilst I filled the two pails at the well. My antiquarian aspirant soon returned with the pick and the spade but reported no sign of the blacksmith himself and all was strangely silent in the forge with the tools left at the door. As we made our way upon the soft turf Robert declared a fascination for the "pleasing embreastment of this Plain" by the many rounded barrows and then demanded that the great bustard should appear before us as I had earlier informed him of the existence of this bird. Any hope of sighting this elusive creature was surely in vain by the amount of chatter and laughter that follows Mr Robert Foster wherever he goes. My companion has also demanded explanation as to why I have a dead snake upon my battered hat. The recounting of this tale also unravelled the tangle of misadventure that has befallen this pedestrian tourist whilst at large in South Wiltshire and

Robert was keen to avail himself of every detail.

"I believe that you would cause less disruption Henry behind a desk at Chalk's brewery in Southwark. We may then all sleep safely in our beds."

Robert and I are both clinging to the shadow of one dark stunted bush with our pens scratching away in unison. The excavation proceeds at a furious pace as we each take our turn with the blacksmith's tools whilst the other empties the brimming pails of chalk upon the ever growing spoil heap. Indeed the blocks of chalk have now increased in size as we delve further into this Plain and these larger pieces can barely fit the pail and must be handled on their own. There is great encouragement also by the discovery of large nodules of dark flint that have been returned to the pit by those early excavators and it is perhaps an indication of what may lie at a greater depth. To my great surprise Robert then related the tale of a piece of common flint and its journey from undisturbed slumber beneath a blanket of chalk to a life of turmoil as gravel upon the river bed or indeed sand upon the beach. "It is only by some great cataclysm that this disruption occurs Henry and indeed is it not hard to imagine upon such a fine day?"

By the look upon my face Robert then stated with mock surprise that he was not an automaton that simply read aloud my letters to his dear Sister. When put in these terms I then blushed beneath my mask of white chalk and upon hearing again my own words and thoughts I resolved privately to never engage upon such stony matters to Miss Sarah Foster.

*

We have dug perhaps for another hour and a further rest is required. Robert's hands have already become raw by the unfamiliarity of using such tools but his good humour appears boundless. "Shall I make a fine antiquarian Mr Chalk? Is my swing just so with the pick and my push upon the spade without equal? To whom should I subscribe to join your most mysterious Order?"

I explained that true antiquarians did not appear until noon and that we were but simple labourers.

I then recalled my curious dream of two days ago that had occurred as I rested beside the pit and I now spoke of it to Robert. Into my slumber had crept the originators of this pit for I could hear the very sounds of their excavation; their chatter and coughing and even a sonorous voice in lilting song. I could smell the sweat of their labour for they worked close beside me and all the while an old man struck upon large pieces of flint with some heavy stone tool. Chink, chink, chink. To Robert's great disappointment I then described the opening of my eyes to find that these ancient miners had become a flock of grazing sheep and the old man a shepherd with a look of disapproval upon his face. As Robert wished to hear more I explained that at night in my bed whilst my bones and muscles ached I have thought or dreamt a great deal about these holes in this Plain. I had one persistent vision that it was not a Plain at all but a forest and that the dormant flint that lay undisturbed beneath its white chalk counterpane was the means to turn a forest into a Plain. "How so Henry?" asked Robert in some confusion. From my mouth then issued a verse or poem and I know not from whence it came;

> Once a forest, now a Plain
> Felled by man, to open remain
> By what means this action taken?
> The source lay beneath the root
> So long in slumber
> This richness beyond all the world's treasure
> A black jewel to spark and hew
> This union of cold stone and warm blood
> To fell a tree
> And split asunder
> To burn and bake
> Toward a new horizon.

I have written down this strange arrangement before it slips away. Perhaps it is after all dreams that cause poetry to occur for there has been no waking thought or chasing about the page. Please forgive this new indulgence my dear Uncle.

*

After enjoying our nuncheon of hard boiled egg with cheese and bread I believe that Robert Foster has fallen asleep beside me. It is hard work indeed and the heavy air in combination with a ferocious sun condemns the labourer to suffer greatly in these conditions. By his knowledge of anatomy Robert has been able to identify the most curious object that has yet been extracted from our pit. It is perhaps sixteen inches in length and is a broad and tapering flange of bone with a naturally occurring attachment of bone at the narrow end that forms the perfect handle. It is the scapula from a large beast of burden and this broad shoulder bone has been adapted to form the most perfect shovel. There is also a small pile of flint axes that lay beside a number of worn deer antlers and I shall make a drawing to record all these objects. One deer antler is assuredly a damaged pick that has been discarded and I have located a number of round holes in the walls of this pit where a bone pick has been punched into the chalk. This is of great interest for it displays the manner in which this pit was dug by such primitive tools. These three holes are aligned and they follow a flaw in the native chalk. We are digging a pit where the matrix of this ground has already been broken into and so are removing loose material. The ancient miners were confronted by a solid geology and have utilised every little help that nature may provide. I wonder how deep we shall be required to dig to establish the base of this pit?

I also believe that with the absence of pottery and other signs of domestic habitation I may now exclude the notion of pit dwellings as a purpose for these many depressions in the ground.

Whilst Robert Foster sleeps I may risk the recording of a conversation that has just taken place between us. He has explained that whilst he has been away from the family home his dear sister has been venturing out upon her own. Concern has been raised by their father, Mr Gerald Foster in correspondence to Robert. Sarah has described her excursions in detail to her father and is determined to continue. I can only cast my mind back to that night in Hindon when I first met Sarah and she had then defied the will of her brother by not staying in her room. Upon that occasion it was the horses in the stables that she had sought to feed but had then become alarmed by the many drunken men on that election night. It was indeed my good fortune that I was able to assist but I can now share in the Foster family's concern by this new display of wilful independence.

Sarah Foster has taken to walking upon her own the steep gradient from the house to the quay. There is an unevenness to this steep street but in that unevenness she has devised in her mind a map that she may read with her feet. The gaps between the buildings are felt by the currents of air upon her cheek and a change also in the sound of the tapping of her stick. She holds herself erect and tries to imagine how she looks to others. Sarah talks to the occupants and visitors upon the street and recognises their scents and coughs, their whistles and clicking heels and even the laboured breathing as they ascend the steep hill. She speaks "Good morning" to the shop keepers as they stand at their doorways but suspects that they are now waiting for her and so changes the time of her walk. In this way different people are met with and life is more haphazard and it is a quiet mischief as she senses this disruption.

Robert Foster has informed me that the purpose of his excursion from the family home is to seek medical advice and expertise into the treatment of blindness. He has travelled to Edinburgh and Liverpool and spent a deal of time in London. Robert informs me that if travel abroad was not so fraught with danger then he would visit every capital city in Europe if he thought that he might gain some knowledge there. I now consider my own churlish frustrations caused by Robert Foster's delay in not arriving at the Winterslow Hut until last evening when I did not understand the purpose of his journey. Whilst Robert has sought high and low for the best medical advice in an attempt to cure his dear sister's affliction (and believes it a fault of science that this cannot be achieved) Sarah is quietly finding her own way in the world.

*

We could achieve no more today and Robert Foster has been unstinting in his labour and interest in my investigation of this pit. He is a true friend and I believe that it shall be a friendship that will endure and prosper. Whilst my face and skin have become seasoned by my exposure to the ferocious sun so Robert's fair skin has suffered and is made bright red. His hands also are torn and bleeding but neither of these things have dampened his spirit for "..progress has been made my dear Henry. Progress has been made."

Upon our weary return to the Winterslow Hut it transpires

that there has been the discovery of some thefts. The landlord has advised that all guests must be diligent in the locking of their rooms for a fob watch has vanished and also a small quantity of money. Robert has suggested helpfully that as I was found creeping about the landing upon his arrival then I should be cast in irons without further ado and the landlord has accepted this proposal with a wry smile. The landlord also informs us that the ailing doctor is insistent that his door must still be left ajar and, as he struggles to sleep fitfully, he should soon witness any intruder no matter what the hour. Robert has indeed offered his services to the ailing Doctor but has been informed kindly that it is a reoccurrence of an affliction that will only abate with rest and darkness.

After a necessary encounter with hot water before dinner, Robert has again returned to my room where he has picked up your slim volume of "A Pedestrian Tour of North Wales, 1805". I explained that it was the reading of this publication that prompted my flight from Southwark in October last, to conduct my own pedestrian adventure. I have read it over and again but more often will read the fond dedication that you yourself have written at the front. To hear it again read by Robert Foster renews the warmth and inspiration that I have gained from your kind words.

"To my dear nephew Henry, may you think of me not as your absent Uncle but instead as a true friend. Distance and circumstance have conspired against us but you will see from this small publication that I am very much alive in mind and body. To the few that choose to turn these pages I shall be Anonymous but to you my Dear Henry I shall be forever your faithful Uncle, James Chalk."

I confirmed that it was to you my dear Uncle that my flow of correspondence is directed when I am embarked upon my pedestrian excursions, in the vain hope that you will enjoy these twists and turns. Robert then asked whether you had indeed reciprocated in the knowledge that your Nephew was residing here at the Winterslow Hut these last few days? I confessed that I had not received word since the arrival of your book in Southwark over two years ago but would not be discouraged. I stated that I sincerely hoped that you are well and in good health but that you are too busily employed and perhaps engaged upon more adventures of your own. Indeed it is I who am at fault for my erratic and irresponsible behaviour and so I do not deserve your interest or sanction.

Tiredness has prompted an early night and out in the hallway Robert has confirmed his unerring support for our excavation. He then stated loudly that the "White hole of Winterslow" would finally relinquish its secrets and that tomorrow would bring great excitement. I then had to ensure that he bridled his enthusiasm least he awoke the guests already in slumber and reminded him to lock his door to the prowling thief.

It is now as hot by night as it is by day and indeed the perspiring landlord exclaimed that what was needed was a good "rattle-round" by which I understand that a storm is required to clear the air. Indeed the pen slips between my fingers as I write and my body is infested by these little black bugs that makes the skin itch so.

Before I attempt the discomfort of sleep in this heat I shall continue with my letter to Sarah for I believe that Robert Foster is anxious to return home despite his enthusiasm for my venture. Once my good friend departs, I shall not linger here beside the busy London Road and must form a plan of my own. I believe that it is time for us to meet again my dear Uncle for too much ink has been spilled in the recounting of my exploits and I know nothing of your own circumstances. Pray send word post-haste if you are agreeable to this meeting after so many years.

Your faithful nephew
Henry Chalk

MY DEAR UNCLE,

Even in the early morn the heat is intolerable and I pray that the "rattle-round" will come soon. Indeed the sky is heavy and the milk at breakfast is turned sour by this atmosphere and everybody complains at this helpless situation. Even Robert Foster appears weary this morning and admits to lethargy. It is as I feared, for Robert has informed me that he intends to depart for Somerset this afternoon. He has been estranged from his family for too long and Sarah has not been made aware of the true purpose of his absence. I have urged Robert to depart sooner but he is insistent that the day shall be spent at the excavation for he does not wish me to work on my own for fear that the walls of chalk may collapse and I should be buried alive. We both sense that we are very close to reaching the base of this pit when its secrets shall be revealed and so Robert has now appeared at my door and we must depart.

*

We are now sheltering from the sun beside the pit but it is no longer the sun that is the enemy for it is the heat and the closeness of the air that is most oppressive. Whilst I filled the two pails, at our departure from the Hut, Robert sought the blacksmith to retrieve the tools but then returned with the saddest news for he has spoken with the blacksmith's eldest daughter. She has informed him that the family had attended the funeral at Winterslow church of her brother Edward who died upon the advent of his first birthday. Indeed we heard the tolling of the distant bell and I now reflect upon the picture of the smallest and plainest of coffins carried by the Father to the grave. Mr Rogers, the blacksmith, has been the most taciturn of men and I think back to Sunday and of his visit to the excavation to ensure that I ceased my labours upon the Lord's day. I now regret deeply my causing the blacksmith to be troubled by this disregard and yet I hope and trust that his faith will serve him well for it is a loss that cannot be easily accepted by a rational mind alone. There are many deep memories that may be stirred by such solemn news and yet I am reminded of the excursion to the Ashton Valley barrow opening in the frozen and faraway month of January at the beginning of this year. It was with great expectation that Mr William Cunnington, Sir Richard Colt Hoare, the two Mr Fenton's and I set out under the threat of snow from Heytesbury to examine the largest barrow beside the Chitterne Brook. I recall now the silence at our arrival as we looked down upon the skeleton of a child carefully revealed by the labours of Mr Stephen and John Parker. This life had not flourished beyond one year and it is a tragedy to consider the burial of a child so young and has it not always been so? The thick and silent flakes of snow soon cast a white shroud upon this pitiful sight and the heaved spoil from the excavation was replaced by Mr Cunnington's men.

*

Robert has been strangely reticent this morning and we have gone about our work both deep in thought. We are now nine feet below the turf by my estimation and the original sides of this pit are no longer vertical for there is an undercutting or even a tunnelling into the native chalk. The steps and platforms that we have created to enable access to this depth require some contortion but this once disturbed chalk appears to hold its form sufficiently. There have been some minor falls of chalk upon the excavator but Robert is concerned regarding the overhang of chalk and questions the certainty of its stability but I can detect no fissures or cracks that might cause this to fall.

*

Robert has now broken his silence. He has announced his future plans and it is as if he has also extracted more from this hole in the Plain than just chalk and flint.

"Henry, I have informed you of my purpose in being away from home but I have since made a further resolution. You must promise me Henry that you will never communicate to my sister the purpose of my absence nor what I am about to tell you."

I ceased my digging at the base of the pit as if to emphasize this pledge. I may now reveal these facts to you my dear Uncle for I have entrusted you with my every detail thus far and I believe that it shall in no manner compromise my pledge to Mr Robert Foster. Neither did I remind Robert that the communication between Sarah Foster and my self is wholly dependent on his intervention. Robert then reiterated the nature of his visits thus far to the eye hospitals in the North of this Country and also to those in our Capital City where he has questioned surgeons and medics upon the subject of diseases to the eye.

"I know not on what scale I may contribute to a cure or to the relief of those afflicted by blindness, but I intend to pursue a career in medicine. I can no longer stand by, my Dear Henry, when I am convinced by all that I have heard and read on this subject that science may achieve a great deal more than a dose of mercury and the application of leeches to the back of the head. I shall do whatever is required of me to achieve this goal and yet I believe that the most difficult of these tasks is to keep this news from my dear Sister as her senses are the sharper for the loss of one."

I resumed for a moment the scraping at the bottom of the pit but my preoccupation with the past and all that is long dead has of a sudden become shallow and worthless by this news. Indeed, is it not obvious? It is the living that require our best endeavour for we can no longer help the dead by the discovery of their intentions.

I then climbed from the pit to shake Mr Robert Foster violently by the hand and declared my wholehearted support for this new ambition. If Robert Foster is to dedicate his life to medicine then I must commit myself to assist in this most worthy and noble aim. My thoughts are akin to a man running that cannot keep up with the speed that he wishes to achieve and his legs then slither about with furious instability. There can be only one solution to the assistance that I am able to give. By necessity Robert shall be estranged from his sister in the pursuit of his studies therefore would Sarah Foster consider me even as a poor substitute for the brother that she loves so much? My current circumstances would not permit any such approach least I return to my London obligations and cease my irresponsible ramblings. It is a course of action my dear Uncle that I believe would gain your wholehearted support. Am I not too young to request of Mr Gerald Foster, the hand of his daughter in marriage?

*

Robert Foster is soon to depart for Salisbury and then via Bridgwater to Minehead. Our minds are racing with the possibilities of these new plans and I have returned to my room with the spade and the pick such is my disorientation. My heart is beating so fast that I believe that it will burst from my chest and I know not how to control myself. I must soon compose myself for I shall now write a brief letter to Sarah Foster. I have torn into many pieces my first letter for all has now changed. Gone forever is the grand poem and tumultuous prose for Robert has described how his sister receives my correspondence. "Sarah does not crave for metaphysics Henry and is happiest when you have your hands in the soil. Indeed earth and Earthly matters will suit very well." I am so very much relieved by this news for my cup of ordinariness doth overflow.

I am to be defeated by the pit for it has retained its secrets. Once Robert disclosed his plan I then escorted him at once back to the Winterslow Hut to prepare for his departure and all thoughts of excavation were abandoned. See how my hand still trembles but I cannot delay further my dear Uncle and must now write to my beloved Sarah.

*

The sky has grown so very dark and Robert has just this minute departed upon the Salisbury coach. The air is thick with the brew of the storm and it growls close by but has not yet begun to rain. I know not what to do with myself and am pacing all about the place. I have a great temptation to return to the pit with the pick and spade for I am certain that there is but a small scraping to be made to reveal the base of the pit. A great flash has illuminated the room and the boom of thunder is fast upon its heels. I can hear the horses fearful in the stables below and the dogs have begun to bark and howl. There is a great excitement and an electricity in the air and I cannot remain cowering here whilst the sky is at war with the earth.

ROBERT FOSTER'S LETTER

Thursday 19th May 1808

MY DEAR SIR,

It is my unfortunate duty, as a loyal friend to your young Nephew Mr Henry Chalk, to correspond regarding an incident that has lately occurred. You will, I trust, forgive me if I delay my own introduction by assuring you that your Nephew is alive but has not yet fully awakened these last two nights. His signs are indeed encouraging and yet your Nephew has received a blow to the skull from which unforeseen complications may arise. I have witnessed before the results of cranial fracture and also the swelling of the brain cavity through the pressure of bleeding from within. Young Henry has also sustained at least two broken ribs but I do not consider that his lungs have been affected for his breathing is regular.

I am aware, through earlier conversation with your Nephew and as his trusted friend, that he has kept you very well informed of his every movement whilst at large in South Wiltshire as a pedestrian tourist. I must also surmise that Henry has made mention of me, for his diligence would not permit otherwise, but I shall now introduce myself. My name is Mr Robert Foster and I hail from the town of Minehead in Somersetshire. My Father is Mr Gerald Foster and my

Mother Mrs Anne Foster. I have also a younger Sister, Miss Sarah Foster. I have of late travelled to the North of England and also to London but I am soon to return home. I am much gratified that Henry should agree to our initial union here at the Winterslow Hut beside the London Road upon my homeward journey. Indeed exceptional circumstances have permitted a close friendship to prosper through the pen alone and we were both anxious to meet in person.

I can anticipate your alarm at the sudden cessation of correspondence from your devoted Nephew and I sincerely believe that he will resume this duty as soon as he is fit to do so. It therefore falls to me to describe, as best I can, the events that have caused the peculiarity of my intervention in your Nephew's affairs. I fear that you must also suffer the rhetoric of one who aspires to a career in medicine rather than that of bold adventurer and antiquary.

It is my intention to be brief although I have often been reminded of my perpetual failing in this regard. I hold little doubt that Henry will have furnished you with ALL the circumstances that have led to an excavation upon the Plain behind the Winterslow Hut. (Indeed, how could he ever resist imparting the extent of his enthusiasm for such a venture?) I too have succumbed to the infection of antiquarianism for I joined with Henry in the digging of this hole. Indeed it is my great regret that I did not remain to complete the task for I should not be writing to you now and Henry would not be laying abed with a bandage upon his head.

After many days, indeed weeks, of fine weather with not a drop of rain to be had, the dark storm clouds finally gathered above Winterslow. I said farewell to Henry Chalk as I departed for Somerset and to this end I was first required to make the short journey to Salisbury riding on the outside of the already crowded coach. I had not travelled one mile before the heavens collided and a great fork of lightning struck a large roadside tree causing a huge bough to crash down before us upon the turnpike. The team of four reared up as one at this terror and despite the great skill of the coachman in attempting to control the horses, the carriage then mounted the steep verge to be thrashed by the hedgerow before toppling over upon its side. All aboard the roof were thrown out with the luggage and those passengers who moments earlier were nestled contentedly on the inside were now very badly tumbled about. Two horses remained mortally wounded upon the road whilst two broke free of their harnesses and fled back to the Winterslow Hut thus raising the alarm. You can well imagine the scene for there ensued a great deal of panic amongst these unfortunate travellers and whilst limbs were broken and heads were dashed, thankfully none were mortally wounded by this calamitous event. The coachman stamped about upon the turnpike and was much aggrieved at the damage to his carriage and the loss of his impeccable record after thirty years of service on the London Road. The passengers upon the inside were extracted and I was able to come to aid of those most in distress as makeshift splints were applied. The most severe cuts were bound by a torn petticoat that had become caught upon the hedge from the strewn luggage to which no lady laid claim. The returning pair of wild eyed horses surely signalled that a disaster had occurred to the lately departed Salisbury bound coach. A team of carts duly arrived to escort the damaged party back down the hill to the Winterslow Hut just as the first splashes of rain turned to a deluge and I have never before witnessed rain of such Biblical proportions. As the sodden passengers either limped or were carried to shelter the carts then turned swiftly about for there was a great deal to remove from the turnpike before night fall. I then requested of the landlord that beds should be made available for the needy and hot water was required aplenty to bathe wounds. A number of guests already in residence were made to double up and the ailing doctor who had been ensconced for some days in a room across the landing from your Nephew had now inexplicably vanished without paying his considerable bill. I cared not for the landlord's defamatory remarks concerning this gentleman, only that his bed was now vacated. I recommended that a doctor should be summoned but the landlord said that I was ".doin' a main good job Maaster Voster Sir,n' doctors be costly."

I had not given one thought to your young nephew until I sent the chambermaid to summon Henry so that he might assist with the care of the injured. She soon returned to inform me that his room was locked and that try as she might he could not be raised. The landlord then provided a key but of Henry there was no sign. As you know your nephew well Sir, you will not be surprised to learn that he had returned to the excavation at my departure. That he was in peril I held no doubt and good fortune saw the arrival in the yard of the blacksmith who had returned from the upturned coach for a second block and tackle. I hurriedly explained my intention and the blacksmith took no convincing to hasten to the excavation aboard his cart. The blacksmith knew his ground and we were soon at the opening to the excavation. I leapt down upon the sodden turf to see the worst of my fears now realised for a fresh fall of chalk had detached itself from the wall of the pit to cover the base of the excavation. The steps and platforms within the pit that had previously offered help to descend the hole were now so slippery underfoot that I required a rope to cling upon that was then lashed to the cart. I called out "Henry, Henry" over and again to which I received no response. At first, with my bare hands, I scrabbled at the fresh chalk throwing it behind me only for it to return to the base of the pit and so the bucket was again utilised. Another rope was then applied to the handle of the bucket to enable the swift ejection of the now slippery wet fill by the blacksmith. The heavy rain continued unabated and I confess that I held little hope that we should find your nephew alive. I now employed a spade to the task and in time I struck metal and indeed I found one of the original tools utilised by Henry and myself. With the removal of more spoil I could determine that the pick and the spade had been crossed and wedged above the base of the pit and I believe they had formed a fortuitous brace to arrest the fall of the mass of chalk. Beneath these blessed tools I first found a pale and cold hand and in this small cavity that had been so formed I then encountered the poor crumpled body of your Nephew and my dear friend, Henry Chalk. Indeed it was the bracing by these tools that had preserved the life of young Henry for without them he would surely have been crushed and submerged in chalk. A small gap had also been preserved at the under cut of the excavation which permitted the air to pass the collapsed spoil. Henry did not stir as I hauled him upright and indeed he was a dead weight but not yet dead. I then placed the rope around him and with the blacksmith hauling and me pushing at the limp form and so he was retrieved from the pit. No sooner had I also gripped the rope to be pulled to the surface then another collapse to the side of the pit occurred to send a fresh smothering of chalk to fill the base of the excavation.

With Henry in my arms aboard the cart we fought the driving rain until we reached the sanctuary of the Hut. You cannot imagine the appearance of your nephew as he was laid upon the kitchen table and indeed the chambermaid fainted as she looked upon this limp soul all soiled with blood and chalk. His pulse was so very weak and he so cold that I called for a bath of hot water to raise his temperature into which he was plunged fully clothed. The landlady protested at my action saying that it was well known that a bath of cold water was best in these circumstances to which I replied that I wished my friend to live and not to perish from an old wives remedy. I was then able to bathe and examine the wounds upon his head still fearful that he may yet expire. His pulse became a little stronger whereupon we quickly stripped and dried him and then wrapped a great bundle of blankets about him. I then bled him only a half a pint as I could not gauge the volume of blood already lost. I wrapped his head and he was then put to bed and I kept a constant vigil upon his living signs. I knew that if he survived the night then he may yet live and I can inform you Sir that it was the longest night of my life.

There were other patients to provide a distraction with window glass to be extracted from cuts and nerves to settle. By the morning a little colour had returned to Henry's cheek and his breathing had become more certain. Indeed there was a flock of maids and female guests at the door who wished to confirm, to their own satisfaction, that Henry Chalk was still alive.

Two nights have now passed since the turmoil of the storm and Henry Chalk is most certainly alive. At first he stirred and upon my examination of his ribs he then moaned in protest. His eyes have opened and a weak smile has been offered to please the chambermaid.

Sir it is now late and I shall resume briefly in the morning before the post departs.

*

It is Thursday morning and Henry is awake and demanding to be fed. Indeed all the patients are on the mend and many have now departed but one gentleman with a broken leg requires very careful transportation and must therefore be a patient patient.

Henry should remain rested for a good many days and I have arranged for his good friend Mr Richard Fenton to ensure the continued care and convalescence at the home of Sir Richard Colt Hoare in Stourhead. Mr Fenton will arrive tomorrow when I must again attempt to depart for Somerset.

I believe Sir, if you will accept the meddling of a stranger, that your devoted nephew would dearly welcome a letter from his Uncle for it would cheer him greatly and thereby aid his recovery. I believe that two years or more have passed since Henry last received word from you whilst the weight of correspondence has assuredly been flowing in the opposing direction to keep the post-chaises busy and the Postmasters in full employ.

I sincerely hope that we shall meet one day and pray forgive my forwardness.

Your humble servant
ROBERT FOSTER

SOMETHING BAD HAS OCCURRED for the chambermaid shows great concern and even the landlord has appeared at my bedside to ask if I am now recovered. I have a dull pain in my head and more so when I attempt to move. There is also a great discomfort upon one side of my chest. Robert Foster is to return shortly and he has promised to explain why I am laying abed with a bandage upon my head and why he is here at the Winterslow Hut at all. I awoke with a compunction to write and so before departing Robert has reluctantly placed the pen, ink and paper at my bedside.

*

I have just opened my eyes to see a large wavering shadow upon the wall. This creature has a long neck and a large beak and it is a most proud and regal bird. The giant head turns warily back and forth but all the while it keeps its haughty pose.

I heard my voice croak a hoarse whisper.

"The great bustard"

In an instant this giant bird took flight as Robert Foster untwisted his hands before the candle.

Robert informs me that he spied this giant bird yesterday as it bathed in the dust upon the Plain.

He has now gone to request some broth for he says that I must eat.

*

It is morning and I cannot recall writing of bustards or eating broth and so it goes. At some moments I feel a charlatan for laying in my bed and then I find that I cannot remember what occurred the previous night.

Robert has now encouraged me to write if I am able for he says that it will assist with my recovery. A blow to the head may scatter the memory and the act of writing will help to retrieve these lost pieces.

*

I believe that I understand a little now of what has befallen me as Robert has again told me the whole woeful tale.

Shall it ever be so? Henry Chalk has caused a deal of trouble. I have kept Robert from a reunion with his family by my foolishness. My dear Uncle, I have found my letter that I began on Tuesday 17th and it has remained unfinished and unsent. Upon reading it again I sense and savour the great upheaval in my heart and yet this can by no manner excuse what then occurred.

Robert has informed me that he has corresponded with you and told of how he found your troublesome nephew laying buried in a grave of his own making. Were it not for the bolt of lightning and the accident to the coach then I would be buried still. Robert Foster has indeed saved my life and how can that debt ever be repaid? He has made light of it and the landlord has spoken of how he also treated and tended the injured passengers from the upturned coach. We are all fortunate for the presence here of Mr Robert Foster.

*

I have questioned Robert upon the bustard for after the storm there must be no dust upon the Plain in which to bathe. He informs me that my excavation has been filled in by two labourers employed to the task before another injury is caused. At the base of the spoil heap lays soil that was not dampened by the rain and so this in turn formed the top crust of the freshly filled pit.

"It was here that I spied the bustard Henry, dancing and dusting itself upon your pit. It took offence long before my arrival and erupted into flight."

I now had two subjects to think upon. The bustard at the very place where I had spent so much time with the blacksmith's tools and the pit itself, now filled in.

*

I awoke in the night and it was not at first the returning memory of what occurred in the pit that stirred me but the recollection of a strange odour. It was the scent of freshly broken flint. I cannot describe it plainly other than it being a faintly malodorous gas. This was indeed a returning memory. From this essence I have been able to reform the puzzle that has so far eluded me. Each time it grows with more pieces attached. As the candle has been kept lit in my room I was able to write down this strange tale. I then delved and burrowed like an ancient miner in search of flint and although the page of night thoughts appeared a mess I have now some notion of what took place.

Upon reaching the excavation I spied the shepherd nearby and he kept a constant vigil upon the heavens for the sky had darkened terribly with thunder and lightning close by. I quickly descended the shaft and then extracted a few pails of chalk to reveal the floor of the pit. If you can imagine, my dear Uncle, I believe that the original pit was bell shaped for it is broader at the base than it is at the top. I then cleared the undercut which required climbing from the pit to empty yet more pails of chalk upon the heap. The shepherd again gestured to the sky and waved his arm as if to sweep me from this Plain. He then drifted on with his flock and of a sudden it was as if the great swollen belly of the storm had been slashed open for I felt a weight of water upon me. I hastened back to the shelter of the excavation but the chalk steps soon turned to a treacherous white paste beneath my feet and I slipped and slithered my way to the bottom.

I then made progress horizontally and in the subterranean half light, feeling with my hands, I found my goal. The miners had removed the thick tablet of flint at the base of the pit and here now was the abandoned face of their excavation. They had dared to go no further as they chased their treasure under the chalk overhang. The seam of flint was perhaps five inches in depth and with the pick I prised and twisted and shattered my way until I had a sufficiently large nodule to inspect. I hauled it back to the opening and I then sensed the faint sulphurous odour of flint. A thick white outer rind remained on one side but the meat of the piece was fresh and dark and was the cause of this, and the many other excavations here, all those years ago. In that watery gloom I recall staring at my own bloody prints left upon the chalky white crust of the broken nodule. I put down the flint to study my hands that soon became awash with falling blood.

Robert has informed me that the pick and the spade were found above my head, thus forming a brace to shield me from the collapsed chalk. Try as I might I cannot remember placing them there nor what happened next.

*

I have now informed Robert of this recollection and he has listened with one eyebrow raised and has resisted interruption. Finally he announced that there was one fact that now puzzled him greatly and to date he had discovered no solution. Not only had the chalk wall collapsed upon me but the rough flint axes, that we had extracted earlier, had also found their way back into the shaft and were found resting upon the blacksmith's tools. Robert said that he had not considered this at the time but after hearing my own account he was reminded of it. "It was as if through the vortex of the storm these fashioned pieces and indeed the larger chalk blocks had been sucked back into the pit from whence they came, before the great fall of chalk. The pit has reclaimed its own."

I must count myself lucky and now shiver at the thought of my incarceration in the chalk. I have indeed offended the spirits of this Plain.

My door is now kept unlocked and I questioned Robert about this fact. He tells me that the threat of the sneaking thief has now passed with the departure of the ailing doctor. Not only did he depart without settlement but fled upon another man's stabled horse during the tempest. I felt pity for those at the Hut who had lost their precious goods at the hands of this sly man for a repeater watch was stolen and now a horse and saddle whilst all hands were assisting with the upturned carriage upon the turnpike.

*

I have this early evening walked slowly to the window and that is adventure enough for this pedestrian tourist. The air is sweet and the sky has become alive with the flickering passage of birds that in my ignorance I cannot name. They twist and turn at a rate that is beyond my comprehension when compared to our own laborious trundling about the place. If the human race could travel at this speed then we would be arriving before we had even considered departing and the world would very soon spin from its axis of that I am certain. These sleek and darting birds live under the eaves of the roof here at the Winterslow Hut for they have constructed nests of mud in which to rear their young.

The land has prospered from the rain and has become green when before this same view was straw coloured. I am pleased also that the bustards are able to dust themselves upon my pit.

Robert has again changed the bandage upon my head and

informs me that he is to depart for Somerset tomorrow. The thought that brother and sister will soon be reunited warms me greatly. I had not given any thought as to what I should do next and it appears that Robert has resolved this matter also. Mr Richard Fenton is to arrive tomorrow at the Winterslow Hut and whilst I deplore the great inconvenience that I have caused I shall be very pleased to see Mr Fenton once again.

MY DEAR UNCLE,

I have enclosed my undated pages for there is some news concealed there amongst a deal of confusion if you should care to pick over these ramblings.

It is now raining again but it is a fresh and steady rain and not at all the same tainted and pent up water that fell to earth upon the night of the tempest.

I took delivery this morning of a small parcel from Salisbury and I could not guess at its content. Upon opening it I am now ashamed by my condition for contained within were two flint hearts that I had ordered from Mr Shorto. They are both set in silver and attached to each is a fine silver chain. One is intended for Sarah and I shall entrust it to Robert to deliver in person whilst I shall keep a duplicate for myself. Mr Shorto has also inserted a note to apologise for the delay and hopes that I shall still be at the Winterslow Hut to take receipt of this order. He explains that "..due to the unavailability of ancient flint workers the task has proved a challenge to even his best craftsmen."

The dark flint hearts appear rippled across their surface and are not polished or smooth like a precious stone. They are indeed perfect and I shall send a note at once to Mr Shorto to thank him warmly and also to wish Mrs Shorto and their young family well. I shall communicate to Mr Henry Shorto, in due course, regarding the nature of my excavation for I believe that it will interest him greatly but I sincerely do not wish to steer him from his responsibilities.

The arrival of this package has prompted the recollection of my pedestrian excursion of late for recent events have become estranged from me since awaking with a bandage upon my head. In my thoughts I followed the progress of my ramble and found either pain or pleasure as the story unfolded. I then turned cold with the realisation that I had mislaid the inscribed spyglass given to me by Mr Richard Fenton. That same gentleman is due to arrive here at the Winterslow Hut at any moment and I know not how to describe the loss of such a precious and thoughtful gift.

*

Robert Foster has now departed and I trust that his journey home will be swift and uneventful. I watched and waved from my window as he secured his berth within the coach and indeed the landlord and landlady were in attendance to bid their farewells. I believe that Mr Robert Foster will always be warmly welcomed here should he ever return. We discussed little at our parting for enough has already been said and it shall not be so very long before we meet again. I believe that we now have a bond that exceeds the need for platitudes or overt displays of civility and indeed one look between us is sufficient to indicate our true thoughts and feelings. As Mr Robert Foster departs so Mr Richard Fenton appears and of a sudden I am now a bed-ridden player in a farce fit for the stage. My friend has already whisked up a flurry of activity with the chambermaid required to plump up my pillows and boots to shave the paltry growth upon my chin. An inspection of my wardrobe has revealed a dearth of respectable clothes and more action is required of the staff here to stitch and sew and make good before my departure to Stourhead. My companion then lifted up the snakecatcher's hat and was about to question its origin but then thought better of it and tossed it to one side before inspecting his hands with some suspicion.

I requested that Mr Fenton should seat himself and rest for one moment from attending to my every need for I dearly wished to inform him of the discoveries made here upon the Plain behind the Winterslow Hut. I have in preparation for this moment made a crude plan of the flint pit to illustrate my excavation. As you will recall my dear Uncle, Mr Richard Fenton is an antiquarian of some considerable association and I was anxious to contribute to the understanding of how our ancient ancestors found and procured the best quality flint for their tools and fire making. I was also keen to steer the course of our conversation to a remote destination and far away from the subject of spyglasses.

At the outset Mr Fenton gave every impression of one who was listening but I gauged that he was in truth distracted for he was quick to resume his pacing about the room. The subject of my quest for a source of quality flint was soon to be replaced by how the curtains appeared threadbare and the furniture worn.

To my great astonishment Mr Fenton then picked up my telescope to survey the view from my window and soon described the appearance of a gentleman who was fast approaching the Hut from the village of Winterslow.

"He walks at a fierce pace Henry and indeed he has a ferocious visage to compliment this gait."

I could not at all comprehend the return of the spyglass but was overjoyed to see it in the hands of Mr Fenton.

Mr Fenton would not permit me to leave my bed and indeed it was to inspect the spyglass and not the subject at the end of it that was my intention. I then sank back into my pillow with some relief and yet a deal of confusion. A smile played across the face of my friend Mr Richard Fenton as he continued in his observation of the approaching stranger. Some mischief was indeed in the air but I did not yet show my surprise or pleasure at the reappearance of my spyglass.

I then suggested that the gentleman who was the subject of Mr Fenton's examination could only be Mr William Hazlitt. I remembered the service that I had provided in the transporting of his letters to the small house upon the hill in the village of Winterslow and explained this circumstance to Mr Fenton. I informed my friend that Mr Hazlitt was an artist and also an author and that I had spent some interesting and instructive time whilst walking in his company. I added that he is also a fierce and uncompromising thinker and I recommended to Mr

Fenton that he might make his acquaintance for I should like to witness their exchanges.

Mr Fenton suggested that it was convenient to study him from afar as too much thinking was to be avoided in his experience.

My companion then felt in his pocket and retrieved a note that he had been given by a gentleman who had scrambled from the London bound coach at the change of horses. "I believe that he was one of your own breed. A pedestrian tourist returning to the Metropolis to prepare and concoct the account of his recent excursion for the press. No doubt it will contain the cream gleaned from all the former tourists and a new syllabub whipped up afresh."

I took this note from Mr Fenton and read it to myself as he then continued to scour the fields, hills and hedgerows.

I enclose it for your inspection my dear Uncle to see if you can make some sense of it for indeed I cannot. I am grateful for the return of my spyglass but I am concerned that the author of this short note appears to know my every move and it is a circumstance that I find most unsettling.

Dear Mr Henry Chalk,

I hereby return your Spyglass, you really should take more care of it but I have profited by your carelessness for it has served me well on my Pedestrian Tour of South Wiltshire. I have of late visited Shaftesbury and also the Glove Inn where I enquired of the landlord whether a loss nearby of a spyglass had earlier been reported. Indeed he informed me that this was so and also of your intention to stay at the Winterslow Hut. The landlord demanded a half crown from me for the imparting of this information with the promise that you should then reimburse the finder of this precious object to the same degree.

My route has been somewhat haphazard. I attempted to ascend the summit of Fonthill Abbey, a place that you know well, but got turned away at the gate. I should like to know whether Mr William Beckford has green eyes for I have read somewhere that this is so? I shall of course embellish my tale with a successful entrance to the Caliph's lair and the mounting of his tower.

I have visited Stonehenge and have parted with a trophy of that place that I shall add to my splinter from Shakespear's chair that I collected on a visit to the great Bard's cottage last summer. I have been treated very badly at the reprehensible New Inn that nestles beneath Grovelly Wood. I met with no charcoal burners or deer stealers there, only incivility. I have also made visits to Salisbury Cathedral, Figsbury Ring and Old Sarum, to Wilton House, Longford Castle, Stourhead House etc..etc..

I shall now away to our Capital City where my tale shall grow before it is submitted to the press. The coachman beckons and so we must depart. I trust and pray, Mr Henry Chalk, that you will make a swift recovery and soon return to your pedestrian adventures.

Gratefully yours,
Mr Pedestres.

Mr Fenton smiled and then collapsed the seven tubes of the spyglass before presenting it back to me.

"I have paid the exorbitant tax imposed by the landlord of the Glove Inn to the bearer of the spyglass."

I then looked about hastily for my purse so that I might instantly reimburse my companion the sum of one half crown whilst Mr Fenton, with great theatrics waved away this requirement. I had not the strength to persist but made a private vow to repay this debt. I recalled to my friend the misery of losing the spyglass and the torment of twice seeing it flashing in the sunlight upon the distant horizon and confirmed my great relief at its safe return

Having amused himself greatly, Mr Fenton then departed to secure some lunch.

And so my time here at the Winterslow Hut is near come to an end. My excavation is now no more than a dusty patch amongst the turf and yet it is to the satisfaction of the great bustard. The trophies gleaned from the pit now languish back from whence they came with only the roughest of drawings made to record their existence. I will now forward my plan of the flint pit to you Sir, for it has escaped the attention of Mr Fenton who has not the correct pince-nez upon his person to view it thoroughly. I now await the return of Mr Fenton and before that I am to settle with the landlord.

There is one person whose warm presence in my heart has not diminished one jot when all else has become unhinged, indeed I long to be reunited with Miss Sarah Foster once again. I have good intentions and great expectations after my discourse with her faithful Brother, Mr Robert Foster, that all may yet be resolved.

*

I am to finish this correspondence my dear Uncle and post it directly. I cannot continue under the escort of Mr Fenton and I must leave quietly upon my own. Mr Fenton duly returned and looked the more distracted and then muttered of Mr William Cunnington who has been in London of late and has reluctantly sat for the artist Mr Woodruff on the say of Sir Richard Colt Hoare but is not at all at ease with his new wig and the excruciating posture and wished to retreat back to Wiltshire to find sanctuary upon Salisbury Plain. Mr Cunnington's portrait is to appear as the frontispiece of the Baronet's great work in the making; "Ancient Wiltshire". Mr Fenton then looked aghast and stated that I was sworn to secrecy on this matter for it is to be a surprise and he should never have mentioned it. He then wrung his hands and stated that there was a subject of a personal nature regarding my affairs upon which he must delay no longer in discussing with me. I knew not what was coming next and it has surprised me greatly. Mr Fenton, under council from Sir Richard Colt Hoare, has made contact on my behalf with the trustees and bankers for Chalk's brewery in Southwark. An arrangement has been made where I am to receive a regular income until the hopefully imminent resumption of my responsibilities at Chalk's brewery. Indeed whilst I resided at the home of Mr Fenton in Pembrokeshire in the winter months and put his affairs in order it was an arrangement for which I received payment from the brewery alone. Mr Fenton hoped that my constitution was sufficiently recovered to withstand this news and he regretted deeply this deception but it was essential to acknowledge my whereabouts to the trustees and to ensure my safekeeping. It was felt that I would not give my sanction to this arrangement and so it was a decision taken without my knowledge but with my best interests in mind. Indeed my sudden departure from Fishguard not a month ago had caused a deal of consternation to all concerned. It was then, with no small relief, that the Baronet received recent word from Mr Robert Foster as to my whereabouts.

"I have promised Sir Richard that I would inform you of this.. arrangement and I do so now..somewhat belatedly..but quite essentially ..before your arrival at Stourhead."

My dear Uncle, I am perhaps too young and vulnerable in the eyes of certain friends and yet I believe that I must be wholly in control of my own affairs.

I have one responsibility before I leave the Winterslow Hut for I must visit Mr Rogers the blacksmith. He is a man of few words and I respect him greatly for his faith and resolution. I wish to apologise for the trouble that I have caused for he has lowered his own child into the grave upon the hill in Winterslow whilst I have been fool enough to bury myself upon the Plain.

I must now hurry before Mr Fenton returns.

Those half forgotten events that occurred upon the night of the tempest will I fear plague me for ever and a day. As I lay helpless upon the floor of the pit with blood flowing from my head I believe now that I saw you there standing above me. Lightning glared upon the wetness of the chalk walls and I had not the strength or inclination to move. I looked up to the top of the shaft at the circle of violent sky and as a drowning man will gather the pictures of his life before him in that brief and fatal moment and so I saw your face illuminated by the storm. This vision had allowed for the passing of years to corrupt your features but indeed are we not both older now?

Enough tragedy has kept us apart and we must repair these wounds whatever their cause. It is my intention that we should be reunited, indeed the omens and spirits of the pit have ordained that this should be so. I trust and pray that you will receive me, my dear Uncle, for I am soon to arrive at your door.

Your faithful nephew
HENRY CHALK.